ALECIA'S CHALLENGE

Also by Sandra Diersch
in the Lorimer Sports Stories series

False Start
Great Lengths
Home Court Advantage
No Contact
Offside!
Play On

ALECIA'S CHALLENGE

Sandra Diersch

James Lorimer & Company Ltd., Publishers
Toronto

Copyright © 2011 by Sandra Diersch
First published in the United States in 2012.

All rights reserved. No part of this book may be reproduced or transmitted in
any form or by any means, electronic or mechanical, including photocopying,
or by any information storage or retrieval system, without permission in writing
from the publisher.

James Lorimer & Company Ltd., Publishers acknowledges the support
of the Ontario Arts Council. We acknowledge the financial support of the
Government of Canada through the Canada Book Fund for our publishing
activities. We acknowledge the support of the Canada Council for the Arts
which last year invested $20.1 million in writing and publishing throughout
Canada. We acknowledge the Government of Ontario through the Ontario
Media Development Corporation's Ontario Book Initiative.

Cover image: iStockphoto

Library and Archives Canada Cataloguing in Publication

Diersch, Sandra
        Alecia's challenge / Sandra Diersch.

(Sports stories)
Issued also in an electronic format.
ISBN 978-1-55277-833-3

        I. Title. II. Series: Sports stories (Toronto, Ont.)

PS8557.I385A73 2011   jC813'.54   C2011-903145-0

James Lorimer & Company Ltd.,   Distributed in the United States by:
Publishers   Orca Book Publishers
317 Adelaide St. West   P.O. Box 468
Suite 1002   Custer, WA USA
Toronto, ON, Canada   98240-0468
M5V 1P9
www.lorimer.ca

Printed and bound in Canada.
Manufactured by Friesens Corporation in Altona, Manitoba, Canada in July 2011.
Job # 66766

For Lynn: Because old friends are best friends.
Special thanks to Chris, Mom and Dad, Rachel, and Kira
for all their help.

CONTENTS

1 TOO MANY CHANGES

"Are you really freaked about tomorrow, Anne?" Alecia whispered to her friend.

"Extremely. Are you?" Anne asked, keeping a watchful eye on Connor, who was reading a notice on the school wall.

"I couldn't sleep last night. Mom says it's just nerves, but I think I'm allergic to high school."

"What are we whispering about?" Connor asked, his voice hushed like the girls'.

"Oh, nothing," Alecia told him, smiling too brightly and moving away. Behind her, Connor laughed.

"You're still all freaky about starting grade eight," he guessed. "I've told you, there's nothing to it. You go, get knocked around by a few grade tens, have your lunch snagged by some grade eleven, and go home. Then you spend three hours doing homework you don't under-stand, have nightmares all night, and start over the next morning. Piece of cake."

"You are no help at all, Connor Stevens. Why don't

you just go away and leave us to our misery?" Alecia asked, checking the grade eight homeroom assignments one more time. There had to be a mistake. She and Anne couldn't be in separate rooms on separate floors, it would be just too unfair. But another glance at the lists proved there was no mistake.

"Maybe my mom will teach me at home. She does work at the school board office, so she should know something, right?" Alecia asked, leaning against the wall dejectedly.

"Will she teach me too?" Anne asked.

"Please! Stop it already," Connor told them. "You will both be fine, I promise. Now, can we please leave? I'm starving and I'd like to get away from this building. I'll be locked inside soon enough."

They walked side by side along the sidewalk. Their Vancouver neighbourhood was a quiet one. The streets were wide and bordered with trees; the houses were nestled back from the road on good-sized lots. Many of the families had lived here for years, although there were newer houses as well, large and grand looking.

On this beautiful August afternoon the air was hot and damp. Alecia wished there were just a few more weeks of vacation. She sighed.

"Are you still whining about school starting?" Connor asked with absolutely no sympathy. Alecia glared at him and he grinned at her, his blue eyes twinkling. He had a baseball cap on, but some of his unruly brown curls had escaped and were hanging in his eyes.

"No, I was just thinking about how quickly the summer has gone by. I can't believe Mom and Jeremy have been married for almost two months already."

"But they were together for a long time before that," Anne reminded her.

"Yeah, but Jeremy lived in his own house — he didn't live in mine. And he didn't leave his clothes lying all over the place and his whiskers in the sink and eat all the Fruit Loops and not tell anyone…" Alecia would have gone on but Connor swatted her on the shoulder.

"He also never practised soccer drills with you in the backyard or took you and your incredibly wonderful friends water-skiing on Alouette Lake, now, did he? And he wasn't your dad before, either, was he?" he asked.

Alecia blushed and shook her head. No, he hadn't done most of those things before he'd married her mother. But she couldn't remember ever living with a man. Her father had died when she was only four, and she and her mother had become very comfortable and settled in their routines. "You're right, as usual. But it's still tough getting used to."

"Well, I don't see why. Jeremy is terrific. And he's good at soccer, which is a definite bonus," Anne told her.

"Speaking of which, did Jeremy agree to coach your soccer team?" Connor asked.

Alecia rolled her eyes and groaned. She had come home from Galiano Island the week before to learn that their soccer coach, Mike, had decided to go back to school, leaving the team of twelve- and thirteen-year-old girls with no head coach. That had been bad enough, but not nearly as bad as the parent group asking Jeremy if he would take over. "Yeah, he decided," she told her friends. "He says he'll give it a shot for this season, see how it goes."

"Thank goodness," Anne said, breathing a sigh of relief. "At least we'll have someone who knows what he's doing."

"Like there isn't anyone else in the whole of BC who knows how to coach girls' soccer!" Alecia cried. She was not at all convinced that having her stepfather coaching her team was a good idea.

They stopped walking when they came to Anne's house. It was probably one of the oldest ones in the neighbourhood. It looked deserted.

"Isn't anyone around?" Connor asked.

Anne shrugged. "Probably not. My mom was going shopping and who knows where Martin is. He's never home." She sighed deeply. "Well, I guess I'd better get in. I'm supposed to clean up before Dad gets home this weekend."

"Do you need a ride to practice tonight?" Alecia asked.

"Yeah, that would be great. Just there, though. Mom

is picking me up after."

"Be at my house at six," Alecia told her. "Practice is at six-thirty."

Anne nodded and headed up the driveway as Alecia and Connor continued walking. "Better not make the coach late for the very first practice," Alecia said to Connor.

"And Jeremy is such a tyrant, too," Connor teased. "Is it really awful having him around, Leesh?" he asked, turning serious all of a sudden.

Alecia shrugged and kicked at a stone lying on the sidewalk. "Sometimes it's a pain, I guess. But Mom sure is happy. And Jeremy is really good to her."

"It's been a real busy summer for you; lots going on," Connor said casually.

Alecia concentrated on keeping the stone on the sidewalk. Ever since she had first learned to dribble a soccer ball, she had practised with stones, or fir cones. The longer she could keep the rock on the sidewalk, the better. Today, however, she placed her foot badly, and the stone went up someone's driveway.

"There's just too much changing. I'm getting all spun around," she said.

"Part of life, I guess. I found a whisker on my chin just this morning," Connor said and turned to show her his smooth face.

"You can't shave one whisker, Connor," she told him.

"And you can't stop more from growing," Connor

replied with a grin and ran off, leaving Alecia at the end of her own driveway.

2 COACH JEREMY

Alecia, Jeremy, and Anne arrived at Berkley Field in plenty of time to unload the car and set up the cones for practice. It was a beautiful, big, all-weather field with benches on the sidelines and permanent goalposts. There was even a building with washrooms. A track and bleachers sat at the far end, closer to the high school.

Slowly the rest of the team arrived. They glanced curiously at Jeremy as they pulled on their shin pads and tied the laces of their cleats. Alecia watched her stepfather self-consciously, wondering how he would act. He had met most of the girls over the past few years at games and practices and he knew how they played, but he had never been in charge before. Alecia had convinced him to wear a nylon track suit instead of the old velour one he'd discovered in the back of the closet, so at least he looked presentable, but she was still doubtful.

"All right, ladies, let's get started," Jeremy said, clapping his hands to call their attention. "I'd like four laps around the field, nice and easy, to get us started." He winked at Alecia as she ran past him and she let herself smile in return.

"It'll be fine," Anne said to Alecia as they moved around the field on their third lap. "No one is expecting him to be perfect, Leesh."

"How can you be so sure?"

"Well, Nancy and Rianne already came and told me they thought he was pretty good-looking. That helps, right?"

Alecia had to laugh. "Nancy and Rianne always judge guys on how they look," she reminded Anne. "I wish the players who count did too, then we'd be fine. Some of these girls are pretty serious about the game. They want a good coach, not some weekend-daddy type."

"Jeremy is not a weekend daddy, Alecia. Come on. And he's certainly got the ability, right? He did play for UBC when he was there."

"We'll see."

"Who wants to lead the stretching?" Jeremy asked when they were all gathered together again. Alecia concentrated hard on the toe of her shoe. If he asked her, she would kill him.

"I will!" Nancy Chapman called out in her ridiculous sing-song voice. She jumped up and smiled warmly. "I do it all the time," she told Jeremy.

"Good grief," Alecia hissed at Anne as she followed Nancy's overly enthusiastic stretches. Jeremy watched silently, a small grin on his face, and Alecia relaxed as she realized he saw straight through Nancy's behaviour. Perhaps he would be okay.

"Partner, Leesh?" Anne asked, tossing and catching a ball with one hand. Alecia nodded, listening to Jeremy's instructions.

"Let's do some drills," he said. "Spread out along the lines and let's see how you are at passing." He clapped his hands and the girls moved off.

"I hate these drills," Alecia muttered to Anne as they found a place to work.

Anne shook her head as she dropped the ball. "You always say that, Alecia," she said, grinning. "Why don't you just resign yourself to them?"

Alecia caught Anne's pass with her foot, steadied it, then shot it back, jogging steadily as she did so. As they ran and passed, the conversation she'd had with Jeremy played over in her mind and Alecia grimaced. He had been far too father-like for her comfort.

"If I agree to do this, I want to have some guarantee that you'll support me," Jeremy had said.

"I'm not sure I want my stepfather coaching my soccer team," Alecia told him honestly.

"I guess that's understandable," Jeremy admitted, "but they've been looking for the past two weeks and haven't been able to find anyone else who is qualified. If I don't take it on, there may be no team."

Alecia leaned back against the couch and looked

at the freshly painted ceiling. She heard the unspoken words — don't let your team down because of your own selfishness — but was she prepared to handle the situation?

"Why can't you just make the decision on your own? Why do you have to dump it all in my lap?" Alecia asked.

"Because I can't coach a team if my daughter doesn't want me there," he told her.

Alecia sighed deeply. "But if I say no, I don't want you to do it, I'm letting the whole team down. So what kind of choice do I have?" she asked.

"Hey, no one ever said the choices we have to make in life are easy ones."

"Fine! Fine, we'll give it a try."

Alecia missed Anne's pass and had to run after the soccer ball. So far things were going well, but then, she reminded herself, it had only been half an hour. There was a whole season left to get through. She looked around the field at the other girls running their drills. There were some good players on the team. Alecia sighed. She would never be one of those.

"Alecia," Jeremy said, appearing in front of her, his whistle swinging from his neck. "You've got to take a couple more seconds to steady the ball before you pass it." He indicated for Anne to pass to him, then showed Alecia what he meant. "See? And lean into it a little more. Here, try it again."

Alecia tried again, and again, until Jeremy was satisfied. He then went off to help someone else.

"He's a good teacher," Anne commented. "I knew exactly what he was saying."

Alecia looked after her stepfather, then shrugged. "He's okay, I guess. At least he doesn't yell across the field at you like Mike always did," she said, shuddering as she remembered.

"Man, I hated that! He was so sarcastic. Jeremy isn't sarcastic, is he? I always felt about an inch high when Mike got that little thing in his voice," Anne said.

"No, mostly he just teases people," Alecia told her, looking around for Jeremy. She wished he would change the drill; she was getting bored.

Almost as if he had read her mind, Jeremy's whistle pierced the muggy August evening, ending the drill. They gathered on the grass around him, sweaty and warm. Alecia found her water bottle and took a long swallow. The little hairs that had come free of the braid she always wore at practice tickled her damp neck and she pushed them away with one hand.

"That was pretty good. Some of you are a little rusty, but that's okay," Jeremy told them, balancing one foot on a ball. "I expect that by the first game at the end of September, you'll all be in top form."

"Or dead," Stacie Hutchins, the team's goalkeeper, mumbled and a few of the girls laughed.

"I doubt that," Jeremy told her, smiling. "But let's

do some work with our goalkeeper, since she is feeling a little out of shape."

"Thanks, Stace," someone muttered good-naturedly as they got to their feet and headed toward the goal, dribbling soccer balls before them.

★ ★ ★

Alecia helped Jeremy load the equipment into the trunk of his car at the end of practice and then she sank into her seat and closed her eyes. She was tired and knew she'd be sore tomorrow, but the practice hadn't been all that bad. And it was kind of nice to see the other girls again after the summer.

"Well," Jeremy asked as he climbed in beside her, "How'd I do?"

"Not bad, I guess," Alecia admitted with a shrug. "You've exhausted me and I'm out of water," she said, shaking her empty water bottle at him. She'd have to bring two next time.

"Then I've done my job well," Jeremy said with a laugh. "Nice group of girls. I think we'll get along very well. As long as you can all get used to my rather nasty demeanour."

"Right, Jeremy."

"You know, Leesh," he said, glancing over at her as they left the parking lot, "you are a pretty skilled player."

Alecia opened her eyes, her cheeks hot. "You don't

have to humour me, Jeremy. I already agreed to you coaching," she said.

"I'm not humouring you, Alecia. I'm sincere. What you need, more than anything, is confidence in your ability and a little less attitude. You have good technique and you're fast. You scored on Stacie a couple of times because you read her well."

Alecia wasn't too sure she trusted Jeremy's kind words. Mike had told her she wasn't "on the ball" half the time, whatever that meant. She looked over at Jeremy. "Yeah, well, Stacie was tired tonight. She just got back from camp this afternoon. Next practice she'll block all my shots, you watch," she told him and closed her eyes, ending the conversation.

3 HIGH SCHOOL?!

Alecia, if you don't hurry you'll be late." The voice rose impatiently over Alecia's dream and she groaned.

"Just five more minutes, please, I'm having a really good dream," she mumbled into the pillow. Her mother pulled the pillow out from under her and threw off the sheet.

"I'm up, I'm up!" Alecia announced, swinging her legs over the edge of the bed. Her long hair fell over her face, shielding her mother from her view. She stuck out her tongue before pushing her hair away.

"Don't lie back down," her mother said firmly and closed the door behind her as she left.

Alecia looked briefly at the clock at the side of the bed. It was twenty after seven. She had a quick shower and then stood in front of the closet, frowning. Finally she pulled out her favourite dress and some sandals and put them on. Then she looked in the mirror, eyeing herself critically. Her blond hair hung almost to her waist, her eyes were green, and she had a little line of freckles running across her nose. Passable, she decided. She turned sideways and looked herself over one more time. Everyone else would probably be wearing jeans the first day at school, but it was going to be hot and Alecia was determined to be comfortable.

In the kitchen Jeremy was reading the paper. He was dressed in his usual outfit of suit and tie. This morning's tie had Bugs Bunny on it, which Alecia guessed meant he didn't have any meetings with clients at the architectural firm where he worked. Alecia thought he looked pretty good, generally speaking. His brown hair had little flecks of grey at the temples, but it was thick and wavy. The beard he had grown on holidays was gone, and he wore his glasses this morning, instead of his contact lenses. She decided she preferred the glasses — they made him look intelligent.

He looked up as she came in and smiled. "All set?" he asked. Alecia stood still for his inspection. "You look beautiful, as usual. Well, have a great first day, kid. And we have soccer tonight too, just to make things even better." He winked at her, folded the paper and left.

Alecia put a bowl, cereal, and milk onto the table and sat down. She rifled through the sections of newspaper Jeremy had left on the table, looking for the comics.

"Is Jeremy gone already?" her mother asked, coming into the kitchen. She was dressed in a pale yellow suit and had her hair pulled off her neck in a loose ponytail.

"Yeah, he just left," Alecia told her. "You look really

nice this morning. What's the occasion? Superintendent of schools coming to visit?" Alecia asked. Her mother worked in the accounting department at the School Board. She claimed to enjoy it, but Alecia had always thought it sounded like the most boring job in the world. She had enough of numbers at school.

"Are you implying I don't normally look nice?" Mrs. Parker asked, trying to look hurt but failing.

"Right, Mom."

"Are you all set? Got everything you need?" her mother asked, pouring herself some tea. She leaned against the counter as she sipped it.

"I guess," Alecia said with a shrug. She was starting to feel nervous again and took a couple of deep breaths.

"You'll be fine, sweetie. You always are. And besides, remember my first day? Nothing can be as bad as that, right?"

Alecia smiled. Her mother had fallen down a flight of stairs and broken her leg on her first day of high school. "Well, hopefully I won't break my leg, but I could do a whole bunch of other things," Alecia said, sighing.

"Don't be too optimistic, Leesh," her mother said with a smile, then she went back upstairs.

Alecia drained the last of her cereal from her bowl and put it in the sink. Then she grabbed her bookbag and swung it over her shoulder. "Bye, Mom, see you later."

"Bye, sweetie! Good luck!" her mother called from

the top of the stairs.

Connor was waiting at the corner for her and they walked on together, picking Anne up along the way. In no time they had reached the school. Barely one word had passed between the three friends since they had met. Alecia felt as though cotton was stuck in her throat; she was desperate for a drink of water.

Anne looked like she was going to be sick. Her smooth skin had a ghastly green tinge to it and her dark eyes were glassy. She kept running her hand through her hair, too, so that it stuck out wildly. They stood together, watching the hundreds of students wandering around, waiting for the bell.

"Everyone looks so nervous," Alecia said at last, pushing the words past the cotton. Berkley Secondary was an imposing-looking brick building. It was two storeys high and the windows were tall and narrow. It was very old and crowded, with additions attached in odd places and portable classrooms lined up in rows at the back.

"That's just because you are," Connor told her. "Relax, everything will be fine. If I survived, you can, so don't worry." Alecia didn't feel any better with his words.

"I wish you and I were in the same homeroom, Anne," she said. Anne nodded silently. She was busy eyeing the hundreds of students clustered around the school.

"They all look so much *older* than us. You never

looked that big, Connor," she said softly.

"That sounds suspiciously like a dig about my height," Connor said, trying to sound hurt, but not succeeding. Anne looked alarmed and apologized.

"Never mind, Annie, he was teasing you," Alecia told her and she calmed down.

The bell rang and bodies began shifting toward the large orange fire doors. The three friends slowly moved with the crowd. Inside the door they waved to each other and each went in a separate direction.

Alecia knew by the number of her homeroom, 223, that it was on the second floor, and she had figured out that the even numbers were on one side of the hall, the odds on the other, and that they went numerically down the hall. But as she walked along, checking the numbers, they suddenly stopped at 219. The next two doors were marked "Staff Room" and the door after that had no number at all. She looked carefully, walked back down the hall and checked again, but there was no 223.

The crowd of students in the hall was thinning out. Alecia started to feel panicky, looking and looking for 223. The second bell rang, leaving her in the hall, late for her very first class of grade eight. Doors closed all along the empty hall and she stood there, wishing she had the nerve to turn around and go home. She would just skip grade eight altogether and start fresh next year in grade nine.

"Can I help you find something?" a friendly voice

asked and she looked up and into the face of a teacher.

"I can't find room 223," Alecia said softly, feeling foolish. It was probably directly in front of her.

"Oh, that one. It's at the very end of the hall on the left side past the staff room. A few people got lost, you're not the only one!" the teacher said and smiled. Alecia thanked her and found the room. Opening the door was a completely different story, however. She was now five minutes late and it didn't look like anyone else was arriving. She would have to open the door and go in all by herself. She hadn't fallen down a flight of stairs and broken her leg like her mother, but this felt just about as bad.

The teacher looked up as Alecia came in. She slipped into an empty desk at the back of the room and wished the floor would open up and swallow her. Thirty pairs of eyes turned to stare at her, but then they turned back to what they were doing and ignored Alecia again. She let out a breath and looked around the room quickly, but she didn't recognize anyone from elementary school.

"You must be Alecia," the teacher said and handed her two sheets of paper. "Here is your list of classes and a blank timetable. We're just filling that out for now."

When Alecia did finally meet up again with Connor and Anne two hours later, Anne and Alecia already knew they had no classes together. Anne looked ready to cry.

"How can that possibly have happened?" she wanted to know as they walked home.

"Never mind, Annie, we will still eat lunch together and walk together and stuff. And I'm sure you'll meet someone to help you with your science homework so you don't fail," Alecia told her, teasing. But Anne was too uptight to take a joke.

"I hope I don't fail anything, my dad would have a fit," Anne said, looking worried. Connor smacked her arm gently.

"Alecia was kidding, Annie. You won't fail anything."

"Well, there was a girl I recognized in gym. She moved in down the block from us this summer. I guess it'll be okay," Anne said and tried to smile.

"Exactly. Hey, how did the big family dinner go the other night?" Connor asked.

Anne frowned. "Oh, it was okay. I wish Dad would find a job that doesn't involve travelling so much. He's gone all week and when he gets home on weekends everything has to stop so we can do stuff as a family. I mean, I love my dad, but he's always hounding me or Martin about something. Last night it was Martin's turn. He got this job over the summer and he was really proud about it. He was supposed to work yesterday, double overtime or something like that, and Dad said no, it was a family day and he'd have to find someone else to do the shift. So then Martin told him he couldn't do that and then Dad told him he had no choice and then Martin said he was seventeen and he could do what he wanted and then Dad said that in this household we'd do what he said and then Martin said we weren't in Taiwan anymore and he was old enough to make his own decisions and then Mom dropped a dish on the floor and they shut up."

"Your mom really dropped a dish on the floor? Did it break?" Alecia asked.

"Yeah, shattered completely." Anne smiled and started to laugh. "It was pretty funny, actually. You should have seen the looks on Martin's and Dad's faces!"

"You two coming over to my house?" Connor asked.

"Sorry, can't. Gotta buy some new soccer stuff. I outgrew my shoes and Mom is taking me to buy new ones. I'll see you at practice, Alecia," Anne reminded her and waved goodbye.

4 ADJUSTED RELATIONS

"Stick with her, Rianne," Jeremy called from the centre of the field. "You've got to stay with your man!" He blew the whistle and they all stopped running. Anne and Nancy collapsed on the grass.

Alecia bent over, her hands on her knees, trying to catch her breath. Their first game was a week Saturday and they were pathetic. Above her, Alecia could hear Jeremy reaming out several players. The Mr. Nice Guy routine had lasted all of three practices. In the last couple of weeks he had become more like a coach and less like everyone's best friend. She wasn't sure which version she preferred.

"Let's try it again. On your feet, all of you!" Jeremy cried and blew his whistle.

They spread out across the field again and tried the play once more. It had been hot that day and the humidity lingered in the air, making everything sticky and close. Alecia brushed her sweaty hand across her forehead and tossed her braid over her shoulder for what seemed like the hundredth time that evening. She should cut her hair, she thought as she ran for the ball Rianne passed to her. She trapped it, steadied it, eyed Laurie, their centre, and kicked the ball straight for her. She ran immediately after the play, keeping one eye on Laurie and the other on Anne, who was her opponent for this mini-game.

Anne was everywhere, it seemed — always right in the middle of every little piece of action and in Alecia's face constantly. Alecia wanted to take a fly swatter and swat her away.

"Better! That was much better!" Jeremy called, running alongside the field with the play. "Stay with her, Rianne; stay with her, Alecia. Don't let Anne get that ball! Block her! Come on, block her — be mean about it, Leesh!" he cried.

Alecia turned her body, curving around the ball, keeping it between her feet as she moved along the line. Behind her, Anne pressed hard, sidestepping constantly, trying to move in and take the ball. Finally she did, and dribbled away triumphantly. Alecia bent over, hands on her knees, and closed her eyes. She could hardly take a full breath and she was dying of thirst. Wasn't Jeremy ever going to blow the whistle?

It rang out shrilly at last and all the girls collapsed on the ground, exhausted. "That's it for tonight, ladies," Jeremy called and grinned as Alecia shot him a dirty look on her way to the bench.

"I have to drop some papers off at a client's house, Leesh," Jeremy said, joining her by the equipment bag. "Did you want to come with me, or walk home with Anne?" he asked.

Alecia glanced at Anne and then back to Jeremy. "I think I'll walk. I see Connor over on the bleachers. Maybe we'll get some ice cream or something," she said. She stuffed the last of the balls in the mesh bag.

"You have homework, Alecia," Jeremy reminded her.

"Yes, I do," she agreed, grinning cheekily.

"I think you had better go directly home and get down to it. You can go for ice cream after the game on Saturday."

"Whatever," Alecia said with a shrug, then grabbed her stuff and headed over to where Anne and Connor were waiting for her.

"What was all that?" Connor asked.

"Oh, nothing. Jeremy was pulling his daddy act, that's all," Alecia told him.

"Are we going for ice cream?"

Alecia watched Jeremy drive away, considering her next move. "I have lots of time to do my homework, right?" she said at last, as Jeremy's car disappeared around the corner. "Hey, and Jeremy said he'd take us ice skating on Sunday, if you like, Anne. It's the first weekend the rink is open," she said in a brighter voice.

"That sounds pretty cool," Anne agreed and then

made a face as Alecia and Connor started laughing.

"Please, Anne! That was awful," Connor said, shaking his head.

"About noon?" Alecia asked.

Anne looked thoughtful for a second. "Could we make it twelve-thirty instead? Mom and I are going to church Sunday morning and the service isn't over until eleven-thirty," she said at last, her voice soft and hesitant.

"You don't go to church," Alecia scoffed. "What is this, some new idea of your father's?"

Anne frowned slightly and shook her head. "No, it's my idea," she told them.

"Well, I think it's great, Anne," Connor said before Alecia could say anything further.

"Yeah well, it's just something I wanted to try," Anne said with a little shrug. Alecia looked from Anne to Connor, but said nothing.

The ice cream parlour, a little family-owned shop only blocks from the high school, was crowded when they got there and they had to wait in line. Alecia felt a slight twinge of guilt as she glanced at her watch, but shrugged it off. It was no big deal, she would get all her work done, she told herself.

"This stuff is worth walking for," Connor said, closing his eyes as he ate.

"It's a good thing the place isn't right beside the school, or I'd be a whale," Anne moaned, licking her chin.

"Yeah right, Annie," Alecia scoffed, glancing at her. She was only five feet tall and slender.

"Well, maybe not a whale," Anne allowed, laughing. "It isn't my fault I'm tiny. It's genetic."

"I should have had a double." Connor popped the last of his cone in his mouth and crunched loudly. "That was too good."

"You aren't going to catch it from Jeremy, are you?" Anne asked as they rounded the corner onto her street.

Alecia shook her head. "We've only been half an hour, no biggie," she said. "It isn't like Jeremy is a dictator or anything."

Connor and Alecia left Anne at her place and continued on alone.

"Why do you do that?" Connor asked suddenly, breaking the silence.

Alecia looked at him, startled. "Do what?" she asked.

"Criticize Anne, the way you did earlier about church," he said. He looked up and caught Alecia's eye. Alecia looked away from his flat, blue stare.

"I didn't criticize her. I just was surprised, that's all. She never talked about church before," she defended herself.

Connor didn't buy it. "You could be a bit more supportive, Leesh," he said. "Instead of always poking fun and criticizing her."

"Who died and appointed you my conscience? Don't I already have two parents? If Annie wants to go to church she can go. No one's stopping her. Can we drop it please? I don't like being grilled by you."

"I'm not grilling you, Leesh. But I could if you wanted me to. Did you want to be marinated first? How 'bout a nice lemony dill marinade?" Alecia laughed and pushed him, and the subject was dropped.

Alecia let herself in the house and went to put away her soccer gear in the garage. She could hear her parents in the den, the television mumbling beneath their voices.

"I'm home," she called as she passed the open door, then hurried up the stairs to her room and the waiting homework. She had barely settled at her desk when Jeremy appeared at her door. She looked up at him, smiling, but the smile quickly fell from her face when she caught his expression.

"Where have you been?" he asked, his lips closing over his words into a tight little line.

Alecia blinked at him, stunned at his tone. "We just got ice cream real quick and came right home," she explained, her heart pounding in her chest. She felt like an insect caught at the end of a pin under her stepfather's stare.

"I told you to come straight home and get started on your homework, didn't I?" Jeremy asked.

"Yeah," Alecia muttered, looking at her desk. Why was he making such a big deal of this?

"Then why didn't you?"

"It was only a half-hour!" she cried. "What's the big deal? I'll start my homework now."

"The big deal is that I asked you to come straight home and you didn't listen. And practice ended an hour ago, not half an hour ago. It is now eight-thirty and you haven't even started," Jeremy said, his voice still tight and angry.

"I could start it if you let me," Alecia told him, wondering where her mother was in all this.

"I really hate that you didn't do as I asked you, Alecia," Jeremy said, not responding to her comment. "Because now I feel like I have to do something about it."

Alecia looked up at him. "What do you mean, do something about it?" she asked.

"What I mean is, there'll be no skating on Sunday and you can tell Connor the movie tomorrow night is off. You're grounded this weekend."

"What?" Alecia stood up, glaring at Jeremy. "You can't do that!"

"Of course I can. I'm your father," he told her and went back downstairs.

Alecia glared at the empty doorway. How dare he treat her like that! He wasn't really her father. It was her mother's job to tell her what to do, to keep her in line, not Jeremy's. He had never punished her before, not even a light scolding. She sat for a long time at her desk, too angry even to get up and storm around the room.

"He grounded me!" she cried later, when her mother came up to say goodnight.

"What did you do to deserve it?" Mrs. Parker asked.

"I took a half-hour after practice and went for ice cream and he got all bent out of shape about it," Alecia told her. "I got my homework done in plenty of time," she added.

"Did Jeremy tell you not to go for ice cream?" her mother asked.

"Yeah," Alecia had to admit. She glared at a crack in her desk.

"So basically you disobeyed him and now you're mad because he punished you? Jeremy has the right to discipline you if it's necessary, Leesh."

"I liked it better when you were in charge," Alecia mumbled.

"Pardon me?" her mother asked.

"I said I liked it better when you were in charge," Alecia said loudly.

"Yes, I can imagine you did. You'll get used to Jeremy, too. I know it is difficult to accept a new person telling you what to do, but Jeremy is your stepfather and the discipline can't be left up to me anymore. It'll take some time, but you'll get used to it. Things can't always stay the same." Mrs. Parker leaned over and kissed Alecia's cheek then left the room, closing the door softly behind her. Alecia stared miserably at the closed door.

5 SEASON OPENER

Alecia did her best to avoid being anywhere near Jeremy. She wouldn't speak to him and refused to acknowledge his presence. At first Alecia had thought he might relent and let her off, but he stuck with his punishment right through the weekend. Most annoyingly, he pretended that nothing was any different than usual. He was polite and even friendly to her and didn't seem to notice or even care that she was icy cold in return. Alecia was sure that her mother was getting mean satisfaction out of the whole thing, which made matters worse.

But she found it hard to stay mad forever and gradually forgave Jeremy. By the middle of the following week their relationship was back to normal. The Burrards' first game was that weekend and practice both nights was brutal. But still, they felt confident that they could do well when they left the field Thursday night. Certainly they were playing better than they had been the week before.

Alecia went to bed early Friday night, setting her

alarm for seven-thirty Saturday morning. The game was at nine o'clock and she had to be on the field for warm-up at eight-fifteen. Mike had never expected them to be on the field until twenty minutes before the game, but Jeremy had other ideas. He insisted everyone be there forty-five minutes ahead of time so they could stretch and warm up properly. He had lined up parents to supply oranges and sport drinks. Alecia thought he was possessed. It was only the first game of the season; there were more important ones to come later on.

Despite getting up in plenty of time Saturday morning, Jeremy was nagging at Alecia long before eight. She came thundering down the stairs still braiding her hair. He held her bag out to her, an impatient look on his face. Alecia ignored him and headed for the fridge.

"What are you doing?" Jeremy cried, glaring at her from the back door.

"I'm having some breakfast," Alecia told him calmly. "You said we would leave at eight and it is only five minutes to."

"I said we would pick Anne up at eight," Jeremy corrected her.

"Please, Jeremy! It is only a very unimportant little game and I'm hungry. Relax. Sit down and have another coffee or something."

"Aren't you guys gone yet?" Mrs. Parker said, coming into the kitchen yawning.

"Please, Mother!" Alecia cried. "I just got him

calmed down. But I'm ready anyway. Let's go, Coach. What are you waiting for?" she said, slipping past Jeremy into the garage.

★ ★ ★

Alecia pushed a hand through her damp bangs and let out a long, frustrated breath. They hadn't even reached halftime yet and the Tornadoes had already scored once on Stacie. Alecia could tell that Jeremy was getting frustrated as well. He paced the sidelines like a caged tiger, calling out directions and shaking his head. She took a deep breath and took up her position as midfielder just behind and between the two forwards, telling herself to focus.

Laurie passed the ball from centre to Anne, who moved down the field with it. Alecia kept up with the play, keeping an eye on the tall, annoying forward from the other team. She had been challenging Anne all morning.

"I'm open, Annie!" Laurie called and Anne sent the ball across the field toward her. Laurie trapped it and moved forward, sidestepping a challenging defender.

"Move in, Leesh, move in," Jeremy called from the side and Alecia, suddenly noticing the opening near the goal, ran in to fill it.

Laurie passed the ball to Alecia, but it came at her high in the air and Alecia panicked. She was going to have to head the ball if she had any hope of getting it on the net and Alecia did not like heading the ball. She always managed to hurt herself, despite all the practice. Sure enough, Laurie's pass came straight for her forehead. Alecia closed her eyes, preparing for the impact, but at the last second she chickened out and moved to the side. The ball landed on the ground beside her and an opposing forward picked it up before Alecia could react. Nancy rushed in to defend the net, barely managing to prevent a goal.

"What was that?!" Alecia heard Stacie yell as the Tornadoes sent the ball out of bounds. "Come on Alecia, make some effort."

"Let's try a little harder out there, Leesh," Jeremy called to her as Alecia ran after the play. She was trying. She just didn't like heading the ball.

At halftime they were tied, one-all. Alecia sat with Anne on the bench and ate oranges. "Hey, Connor showed up. What do you know about that," Alecia said, indicating Connor standing with her mother on the sidelines.

"Wow," Anne said, smiling. "What does that make, three games in four years?"

The whistle blew and both teams took up their positions on the field for the second half. Just after the kickoff, Allison intercepted a pass and ran with it. She was an excellent runner and moved down the field easily until a defender from the other team tackled her. The defending player came up with the ball as Allison went down on one knee then rolled over on her side.

Instantly the referee's hand went up and play stopped. By the time Alecia got across the field, Allison was standing up again and shaking off the offers of assistance.

"You okay?" the referee asked and Allison nodded. "Take the direct kick," he said, pointing at Allison with his head.

Allison kicked the ball directly on goal, but the goalkeeper caught it and punted it back down the field. One of the Burrards' forwards managed to intercept a pass between two opposing players and dribbled back down the field. Alecia and Rianne were both open for her pass but Rianne caught it and kicked it at the goal. This time it went in and a cheer went up around the field.

The rest of the game went by quickly and at the end of the ninety minutes, the Burrards were ahead by one goal. The team gathered together around Jeremy, ready for the post-game lecture they had always received from Mike, even when they won.

"Good job! It's always nice to win the first one," Jeremy told them, smiling. "We'll go over the game at practice on Tuesday. You're all hot and tired now. Go home and enjoy the rest of your weekend. But think about your own play and how you might have done things differently."

6 ENTER MONICA

Alecia had a doctor's appointment first thing Monday morning and was late getting to school. Her mom dropped her off near the bike racks. Alecia waved as her mother drove away, then turned and headed for one of the side doors. As she passed the track, members of a gym class ran past and she paused to watch them running, thankful it wasn't her. Two girls were jogging toward her on the track, giggling as they ran. The girl with the shoulder-length black hair looked up at her and waved. It was Anne. The girl she was running with looked up and smiled in Alecia's direction. As they rounded the track, Alecia kept watching them. The girl looked familiar. She had long, dark hair and she was taller than Anne. Alecia tried to remember where she knew her from as she pulled open the door and went inside.

She was putting her clarinet together in band class later that day when she happened to look up just as Anne's running partner came into the room, carrying a flute case. She was laughing loudly and as she laughed, she flipped her hair over her shoulder. It went swinging down her back in one long, dark sheet and bounced as it fell into place. Then the girl spotted Alecia and smiled broadly.

"Hey! Isn't this funny? Here we are in the same band class all term and Annie and me are in gym together and we never knew it! What do you play, the clarinet? I thought about the clarinet but I don't like reed instruments, really. What I really want to play is the trumpet, wouldn't that be great? I think the trumpet would be great to play, especially since I'd probably be the only girl with a whole lot of boys. You should join me. We'll tell Mr. Bryan that we want to change instruments." The girl stopped talking for a second but Alecia could think of nothing to say. She was exhausted just listening to her.

"Oh! How incredibly rude of me! You must think I'm thick or something. I'm Monica Jenkins. Anne told me your name is Alecia. I like that name. I had a doll named Alecia once, a real nice one too, with a porcelain face and tiny porcelain hands and feet. She had the most incredible gold curls. Your hair is kind of straight — pretty though. I like blond hair. I wish mine wasn't so dark. Well, there's the bell, guess I'd better get set up, eh?"

Alecia had difficulty concentrating on the lesson. She couldn't quite believe it. How could Anne like this

Monica person? She went on and on about absolutely nothing and she was *loud*. Everyone in the room was looking at them as they were talking, or rather, while Monica was talking, and she flipped her hair every time she laughed, which was often. Alecia shuddered.

After band, Monica left the room quickly and Alecia breathed a sigh of relief. She really didn't want to talk to the other girl, she'd had enough before class. Alecia grabbed her case and music and headed out the door. Monica was waiting for her in the hall, with a huge grin on her face.

"This is so completely hysterical," the girl said as they walked down the hall together. "I can't wait to tell Annie. We'll all have to get together sometime. It's just so amazing that you and me never found each other. I've seen you, but you know how it is, you get busy and stuff happens.

"I think Annie is such a neat kid, don't you? You guys must be the greatest of friends. Annie has been so terrific to me since I started school here, you know, showing me around, helping me with stuff. She's so smart! I tell her all the time she is such a brain. But I guess you knew all that! You've been friends since grade four or something, she said. Next year we want to take choir together. I used to sing, at my old school, but I didn't sign up for it this time. I've heard Annie sing, she has a great voice, absolutely great. But you probably know that, too! Listen to me telling you about your best friend!" Monica laughed and paused for a breath and Alecia took advantage of the silence to say goodbye as they came up to her locker.

Anne was alone when Alecia met her after school that afternoon. Alecia had been half afraid Monica-the-Hair-Flipper, as Alecia had started thinking of her, would be with Anne, but she was nowhere to be seen.

"So, you knew Monica from band?" Anne asked casually as they started off down the sidewalk.

"No. I didn't know she existed before today," Alecia said.

"She remembered you from band right when we saw you. She didn't know your name though. Did you talk to her? She's really nice, friendly."

"She never shuts up, Anne! Oh my God, she talked my ear off, and what is with that hair flipping thing? It nearly drove me batty," Alecia cried.

"It's just that you don't know her very well yet. If you get to know her I know you'll like her." Anne smiled, nodding, but Alecia doubted she would ever like Monica.

"Well, whatever. I'll see you later at practice, right? It's earlier tonight 'cause it's getting so dark," Alecia reminded Anne as they arrived at her house.

"Sure."

"Say, isn't that your dad's car?" Alecia asked, pointing to the dark blue Toyota parked in the driveway.

"I guess he got home earlier than he expected,"

Anne said dully, frowning at the parked car. "Anyway, I'll see you a little later," she said and headed up the path.

It was grey and cool outside during practice and Alecia was glad she had worn her long-sleeved jersey and track pants instead of her shorts. Many of the other girls shivered even after the run and stretching drills. The ground was damp from the recent rain and everything felt winterish.

"Why can't we play inside?" Anne whined as they gathered around Jeremy after warm-up. "It's too cold out here."

Alecia looked at her friend in surprise. Anne never whined and complained, especially about playing soccer. "What's up with you Annie?" she asked in a whisper.

"My dad found a science test," she whispered back. "He wasn't happy about the mark. He said maybe other things were interfering with my studying and that maybe we should examine my extra-curricular activities."

"I'm sorry Annie, that's lousy," Alecia said, unsure what else to say to make her friend feel better. "Are you okay?"

"Yeah, I will be. I wish I'd worn a warmer sweater, though. When do we start practising inside?" Anne asked. "And why does everything have to get so complicated?"

"Who knows? Come on, let's go do drills together, get your mind off it," Alecia suggested.

It wasn't the greatest practice they'd ever had. It started to drizzle halfway through and the girls were soon drenched and cold. Alecia had to bite her tongue to keep from complaining as much as she wanted to. She looked longingly at the car in the parking lot, day-dreaming about the warmth and dryness inside it. As a result, she was hit by the soccer ball when she didn't see Rianne's pass coming.

"Hey!" she cried.

"Hey yourself!" Rianne yelled back. "Pay attention to the game, Leesh, and you won't get hit."

"I was paying attention."

"You were not! You were staring off into space, as usual. Why do you bother coming at all? Huh? You miss passes and you give the ball up to the other team," Rianne said, breathing heavily. The two girls were glaring at each other when Jeremy appeared.

"What's going on?" he asked.

"Alecia is daydreaming and missing passes again," Rianne told him, throwing Alecia a dirty look. Alecia fought the urge to stick out her tongue.

"Alecia, you've got to pay attention. Keep your mind on the practice or you'll get hurt."

"Whose side are you on, anyway?" Alecia muttered as Jeremy walked away again, blowing his whistle.

"Come on, team," Jeremy called. "Another ten

minutes and we're done."

"Oh hurray," Alecia muttered, lining up as the ball was kicked into play by Stacie. "I might still be alive by then."

She was still alive when Jeremy called time but she felt like a drowned rat as she removed her soggy shin pads and found a towel. Beside her, Anne was busy shoving things into her bag, muttering under her breath. Alecia ignored her, she was in a bad enough mood herself.

"You guys practise outside?" a voice asked and Alecia spun around to see Monica standing warm and dry under a big umbrella. She grinned at the two wet girls. "I would have thought you'd be inside by now. Hey, want to use my umbrella?" Monica offered, and then laughed at herself and flipped her long hair back from her face. "Like it'll do any good now, eh Annie?"

To Alecia's complete amazement, Anne laughed. "What are you doing out here?" she asked.

"Oh, just decided to have a bit of a walk. Thought I'd catch a bit of your practice. I'm not big on soccer myself."

"It can be kind of a pain," Anne agreed, amazing Alecia again. Anne lived for soccer and had done ever since Alecia had met her five years before. She stared at her friend.

"You know, Anne, Jeremy is waiting for us and it is kind of wet out here," she said quietly, swinging her bag over her shoulder.

"Yeah, I'm coming. That was really great of you to come by, Monica," Anne said, turning to the other girl. "Do you want a ride back home?" she asked, and Alecia glared at her.

"No, thanks anyway," Monica said before Alecia could say anything. "I was actually also going to the store for my mother. You know how parents are, eh? Always capitalizing on opportunity. Mom sees me with the umbrella and a coat on and says, 'You're going out? Would you just run past the store and get some milk?' So now I'm going to soccer practice and to the store. Well, I guess I'll see you tomorrow. Bye Alecia," Monica said with a little wave and turned away.

"I get exhausted just listening to her talk," Alecia said as she and Anne walked to the car. "And what's with soccer being kind of a pain? You love soccer! You never complain about the weather, or the cold, or the mud, or the games, or anything!" Alecia went on, throwing her bag in the trunk. It was warm and dry in the car and she sank gratefully into the front seat. Anne climbed in behind her and clicked her seatbelt.

"I guess I was just having bad day," Anne explained and didn't say another word the whole way home.

7 ENTER LAURIE

"Wanna go to the movies tonight?" Connor asked.

"What do you want to see?" Alecia asked, putting down the textbook she had been reading. They were in Connor's bedroom doing homework. Outside a cold, wet October afternoon slowly rolled past. Today had been a professional day, no school. Of course every teacher had given out plenty of homework to keep their students out of trouble, so it didn't really feel like a holiday.

"Oh, I don't know, anything. I just feel like going to the movies. Do you wanna go?" he asked again.

"Sure, I guess. Want to ask Anne, too? She would probably like to go."

"I don't think she can, some youth group thing at her church or something," Connor said.

"What youth group?" Alecia asked with a frown. "Anne doesn't belong to a youth group."

"I guess she does. She was telling me about it the other day. Didn't she tell you?" Connor asked.

"No, she didn't. Oh well. Whatever. Who's driving?" Alecia asked, changing the subject. She was annoyed, though, that Anne would tell something to Connor and not to her.

★ ★ ★

There was a large crowd gathered outside the theatre by the time Connor's dad, Mr. Stevens, dropped Alecia and Connor off later that night.

"Is this movie any good?" Alecia asked, looking up at the posters that lined the wall.

"I don't know. Critics are divided," Connor said.

"Is that how you make your opinions? From what movie critics think?" Alecia asked, stuffing her hands in her pockets.

"Well, how else? I certainly wouldn't listen to anything *you* told me — you have zero taste."

"Thanks a lot. And besides, that's not true. I have excellent taste. So hey, tell me what Anne said about the youth group thing," Alecia asked. She had been thinking about it all afternoon.

"Not much to tell. She said there was a youth group at the church she and her mom have been going to and someone had asked her if she was interested in joining. She was, and so she's going tonight — I think it's tonight anyway — to see what it is all about."

"I don't understand why she would want to join

something like that. We do stuff together on the week-ends. Already she's out every Sunday morning, and she's talking about church this and God that all the time," Alecia complained.

"What's the big deal? If she wants to go to church and belong to a youth group, why should you care so much? You should be glad she found something she likes. She can't only do what you like, you know," Connor said.

"We don't only do things I like, for your information. And she can do what she wants. I don't know why she didn't tell me though," Alecia said as the line started moving.

"Maybe because you criticize her," Connor suggested.

"I don't criticize her!" Alecia said, trying to keep her voice down. Sometimes Connor could be a real pain. He shrugged and said nothing as the man took their tickets and pointed out their theatre.

They found seats near the back, so they could talk and not disturb anyone. Then Connor went to get pop-corn and something to drink. While he was gone, Alecia looked around the quickly filling theatre. Several rows down, she recognized Laurie Chen, the centre on the Burrards. Alecia grinned and was about to call Laurie's name when Connor appeared.

"Hey, miss me?" he asked, slipping into his seat and handing her a box of popcorn.

"Not a chance. I just noticed Laurie's here," she said, taking her box of popcorn.

"Laurie from soccer?" Connor asked, peering around for her.

They were both staring at the back of Laurie's head when the girl suddenly turned around. She grinned when she noticed Alecia and then slid out of her seat and came back.

"Hey, what a surprise," Alecia said and quickly introduced Laurie and Connor to each other.

"Haven't I seen you at games sometimes?" Laurie asked, helping herself to Alecia's popcorn.

"It's likely. I'm a terribly supportive friend," Connor told her.

Laurie laughed. "I bet. Say, you up for that game this weekend, Leesh?" she asked, tucking a piece of long, dark hair behind her ear. "The Rocketeers are the best in the league right now. I sure hope we're ready for it."

Alecia groaned and slumped back in her seat. The previous year the Rocketeers had taken the district championship. They were large and fast and very good at taking advantage of their opponents' mistakes. The Burrards had never managed to win against them.

"I hate playing that team!" Alecia said miserably. "Their forwards are all the size of Clydesdales."

"Well, wear lots of protection. Better go. Nice meeting you, Connor. See ya 'round the soccer field, okay?" Laurie said with another laugh and went back to her seat.

"She's nice, eh?" Connor said, watching Laurie as she slid into her seat.

"Sure."

"I bet she's really good on the soccer field. She's so tall," he went on.

"She's pretty good," Alecia agreed, turning to look at her friend. "You've seen her play, Connor. You know how she plays."

"I guess I never noticed her before, that's all."

Alecia laughed. "Never noticed Laurie? She's the tallest player on the team and the prettiest. How could you not notice her?" She laughed again and straightened around in her seat as the lights dimmed. "Now shut up and let me watch the movie."

★ ★ ★

"So, Laurie's the centre for the Burrards, eh?" Connor asked as they settled in the back seat of Mrs. Parker's car after the movie.

"Yeah."

"She's so tall, she must be really good, I bet," Connor went on.

"What's with the sudden interest in our team centre?" Alecia asked, turning to look at him.

"No reason, just wondering," Connor told her, and looked out his window.

Alecia stared at the back of his head for a couple of

seconds, a puzzled look on her face, then shrugged and turned around. After they dropped Connor off at his house, Mrs. Parker turned to her daughter.

"Why don't you climb into the front seat? Then I won't feel like a chauffeur," she suggested. "Would you like to go shopping tomorrow?" she asked, backing down the driveway.

"What for?" Alecia asked as she buckled her seat belt.

"Well, Jeremy's birthday is coming up and I thought you and I could go together and find him something. And you could use some new clothes, and maybe a new bra."

Alecia blushed furiously and stared out the window.

"What? Did I say something wrong?" her mom asked when Alecia didn't answer her.

"I don't need a new bra," she mumbled.

"You're growing, Alecia. You need a bigger size. Does it embarrass you when I talk about bras and stuff, is that it?" her mother asked. Alecia wished the car would hurl itself into a telephone pole. Instead, her mom pulled into the driveway and parked the car in the garage.

"Can we drop the subject, please?" Alecia asked, pushing her door open and climbing out as quickly as she could. Her mother followed her into the house and put her purse on the counter.

"Alecia, stop for a second and look at me," she said.

Alecia turned around and glared at her mother. "What is wrong? Will you talk to me please?"

"There's nothing to talk about. I don't want to go shopping for — for anything," she said. "You can get whatever you want for Jeremy's birthday, just give me a card to sign."

"I know you don't mean that. Jeremy would be terribly hurt if you didn't give him a gift. It's his first birthday as your father. If you don't want to go shopping for *stuff*, we won't. I'll pick some out for you to try on at home. But you better get used to the idea, Miss, because they don't just materialize out of thin air." They stood looking at each other.

"I'm tired of things changing all the time," Alecia said at last, picking at her fingernail.

"Oh that's what this is about," her mom said softly, coming over and putting an arm around Alecia's shoulders. "I know you aren't big on change, Leesh. But it happens anyway."

"Well, it shouldn't. Mothers getting married and people going to youth group meetings and church," she paused, not sure what she wanted to say next. Her mom squeezed her tightly.

"I'm sorry you have to be thirteen, sweetie. If I had any say over it, you would skip the next five years altogether," she said, and Alecia smiled in spite of herself.

"Sounds good to me. I wouldn't mind being eighteen, then I'd be finished school."

"Yeah, well, one day at a time. Do you want to talk about all that stuff you just spewed at me?" she asked but Alecia shook her head.

"No, I think I'll just go to bed and hide my head under my pillow," she said, and headed slowly for the stairs.

8 BIG MOUTH

"Turn it off, please, I'm drowning!" Stacie Hutchins cried, turning her face toward the grey blanket of sky above her.

"I think a duck has taken up residence in my hair," Laurie added, shaking her head. "Thinks it's a swamp or something."

"That's enough, ladies," Jeremy called, but Alecia could hear the laughter in his voice.

It was pretty disgusting. Rain had been pouring down on them throughout the first half of the game against the Rocketeers and showed no sign of stopping as the referee blew his whistle for the second half. Alecia sighed heavily and rubbed at her damp face with a towel.

"Remember what we talked about," Jeremy called to them as the starting lineup ran half-heartedly to their positions. "FOCUS!"

"Your mother looks nice and dry, Leesh," Nancy said as they crossed the field together. "Do you think she'd lend me her umbrella and raincoat?"

"Not a chance. I saw Jeremy go over there a minute ago and she just pushed him away. Mom takes after me, she can't stand getting wet," Alecia told her.

"Why do we play this game?" Anne asked. They were lined up now, waiting for the centres to take position and the referee to start the play.

"I play 'cause you do. Why do you play?" Alecia shot back with a smile.

"I don't think I know anymore," Anne answered slowly, then turned as the whistle blew, leaving Alecia staring at her wet back.

She had no more time to wonder at her friend's strange comment, however. The break had given the Rocketeers renewed strength and it took Alecia and the rest of the Burrards every ounce of concentration to keep their opponents from scoring on Stacie. The Burrards were playing well as a team. Several times, when she glanced at the sidelines, Alecia saw Jeremy nodding his approval at a play well made.

Finally they reached the last five minutes of play. The Rocketeers had scored the first goal in the first half of the game and despite their best efforts, the Burrards never managed to do more than tie when Nancy had taken a penalty kick earlier in the second half. It looked as though 1–1 would be the final score.

Alecia was impatient for the game to be over so she could get dry and warm. She was hungry too, and tired.

Hoping Jeremy would pull her and substitute another player, she had been staying close to the edge of the field near the centre line when she heard her name being called.

"LEESH!"

Alecia glanced up and saw that Anne had the ball and was preparing to pass it to her. Before she had a chance to react the ball was there. She kicked at it wildly and sent it flying across the field, directly to a waiting Rocketeer. The Rocketeer trapped it and in another second they had scored, winning the game 2–1.

"I don't believe it!" Rianne cried as they left the field.

"Who do you play for, Alecia? The other side?" Stacie asked, throwing her gear down on the bench. She glared at Alecia.

"What? She caught me off guard," Alecia defended herself, but her excuse sounded weak even to her own ears. She moved to get her bag.

"You weren't paying any attention! You were hanging around the sidelines waiting for the whistle to blow," Stacie accused her, blocking Alecia's path. The other girl was the same height as Alecia, but stronger, angry, and intimidating.

"Cut it out, girls. Stacie, go get dried off," Jeremy said, interrupting them. He waited until Stacie had walked away, still muttering, and then turned to Alecia.

"What's going on, Alecia?" he asked, folding his arms across his chest.

Alecia fixed her eyes on the whistle hanging around his neck. She didn't want to look him in the eye. "Nothing," she mumbled.

"You've been slacking off, whining, and complaining for days now. You're not pulling your weight at practice and you're not helping at all in games. You threw away Anne's pass because you weren't paying attention to the play."

"I try my best!" Alecia cried, looking up at her stepfather. Why was everyone on her case all of a sudden?

"No, you don't," Jeremy said, his voice still firm. "And it isn't fair to the rest of the team. I'd advise you to pull it together, Alecia." He looked at her for a second and then he moved away, calling out orders to the other girls. Alecia watched him go, angry and embarrassed. She looked around for Anne, needing someone to say something nice, and finally spotted her further down the field talking with a tall, broad-shouldered boy Alecia had never seen before. Alecia watched, curious, as they said goodbye and Anne came back to get her gear.

"So who was that you were talking to?" Alecia asked as they threw their bags in the car and climbed in.

"Just a boy I met at youth group last night," Anne said, blushing beet red. She turned to look out the window.

"Just a boy? A boy who makes you blush? Do tell, Annie!"

"His name is Tyler. We talked at the meeting and he sings in the choir. He's real nice."

"Annie has a crush!" Alecia said with a giggle, elbowing Anne in the ribs.

"Don't tell anyone, okay?" Anne begged as Jeremy climbed in the front seat and closed his door with a bang.

"I don't know, Annie, this is pretty good stuff," Alecia said slowly, glancing at her stepfather.

"Promise, Alecia!" Anne insisted and finally Alecia nodded, crossing her heart with her fingers.

"Okay, good," Anne said, satisfied.

★ ★ ★

Alecia was at her locker Monday morning, trying to find a book, when she heard a familiar laugh behind her. She spun around, peering down the hall. She spotted Anne walking along, and beside her was a very tall, very muscular guy. She was laughing at something he said and they walked right past without noticing Alecia. Alecia watched them until they went around a corner and disappeared. So that was Tyler, she guessed. Well, well. Anne certainly had good taste, she thought to herself as she closed her locker and went to her next class.

"So Annie, who's the guy I saw you talking to this morning?" Alecia asked casually as the three friends walked home from school that afternoon.

"I don't know who you are talking about," Anne mumbled, turning red.

Connor looked at them curiously. "Oooh, Annie, do tell," he said, in a high, little girl voice.

"It wasn't anyone important, just somebody from choir. He was telling us a joke."

"Us?" Alecia asked. "I only noticed you with him. Was that Tyler?" she persisted, ignoring the look her friend gave her.

"Yes, his name is Tyler."

"Who's Tyler?" Connor wanted to know. Alecia filled him in as Anne stared at her feet. "Anne. Why do you keep these things from me?" he asked, shaking his head sadly.

"I asked you not to say anything, Alecia," Anne said quietly, looking up. Alecia felt twinges of guilt in her stomach.

"I was just teasing you, Annie," she defended herself. "Don't be so sensitive. There's nothing wrong with having a crush on someone."

"I asked you not to say anything," Anne said again and ran off. Alecia stopped walking and stared after her.

"Why'd you do that?" Connor asked.

"What do you mean? You were just as involved as I was!" she yelled at him.

"I didn't know she asked you not to say anything to me! *You* were the one who blabbed in the first place. You better go after her and apologize."

"Apologize yourself! She doesn't need to be so sensitive," Alecia insisted.

"You shouldn't be so *in*sensitive, Leesh. How would you have felt if I had told her about some guy you like?" he asked, looking at her seriously.

"I don't like anyone, so it doesn't matter how I would have felt."

"Get the point, Alecia. You're nasty, and thoughtless," Connor said bluntly.

"Sometimes I really can't stand you, Connor Stevens," Alecia said, furious and embarrassed.

"Why not? Because I tell you the truth?" he asked.

"No, because you're a pain in the neck." She flung the words at him and walked away.

"Great Alecia, just run off. Can't you ever argue like a normal person? My sister is more fun to fight with than you," Connor called after her.

"Then go fight with your sister. Go embarrass her with her latest boyfriend or something," she called back, spinning around again. She was so angry she wanted to hurt him, expose him like he was doing to her. "What about Laurie?" she said, suddenly. "Maybe Anne would feel better if I told her all about the little crush you've developed."

Connor glared at her, his face flushing a deep red right up to his hair line. "I don't know why Anne and I stay friends with you. You can't keep secrets and you aren't a nice person," he said, his voice tight with anger.

"I'm getting tired of being lectured to by you. You think you're perfect, always telling me when I do something wrong, but you're not. What do you do, wait around for me to do something wrong so you can tell me about it?"

"I don't have to wait long, do I?" he asked.

Alecia was stung by his words. She felt tears come to her eyes and blinked them away quickly. Why was he being so mean?

Somehow they had arrived in front of her house while they had been arguing and they stood there, looking at each other awkwardly.

"I think I'm going home," Connor told her.

"I think you'd better," she said. At that moment she didn't care if she never saw him again.

★ ★ ★

Alecia walked to school alone the next day. Connor wasn't at his corner and Anne wasn't at hers. She saw Anne, with Monica, enter the school grounds just as Alecia got to the crosswalk. She sighed deeply. She knew she had to apologize, especially if Anne was going to become best friends with Monica just because they'd had a fight!

Luckily, Anne was alone at her locker when Alecia arrived a few minutes later. She leaned against a door and cleared her throat, waiting for Anne to look up before she forced herself to speak.

"I ... I wanted to say I was sorry for teasing you about ... you know ... in front of Connor." She spoke quickly, getting it over with as soon as possible.

Anne looked at her silently for a long while. "You promised you'd keep it to yourself, Leesh," she said finally.

Alecia took a deep breath and let it out slowly. She was so bad at saying she was sorry! Nothing she said ever came out the way she intended. "I know. I made a mistake. Will you forgive me?" she asked, her face creased in a worried frown.

Anne looked up. It seemed like forever before she finally nodded. "Yeah, I forgive you," she agreed with a small shrug.

"Okay, good. Friends again?" Alecia asked, relieved.

"Sure, friends again," Anne said.

Alecia wasn't so sure it would be that easy with Connor. Still, the empty pit in her stomach was very unpleasant and she knew the only way it would disappear was if she smoothed things over with him.

They found each other at their usual meeting spot at lunch and Alecia was spared having to say anything because Connor spoke first.

"Hi. Don't walk away or I'll bug you until you listen to me, okay?" he said. "First of all, I'm sorry for my incredibly rude and insensitive remarks yesterday. Second, I accept your apology for whatever you might have said to hurt my delicate feelings and third, can we be friends again? I miss you."

Alecia had to fight down an urge to laugh. Connor was much better at apologizing than she was.

"I apologized to Anne for what I said and we are friends again, and I promise to be more *sensitive* from now on, okay?" she said, glad that they were talking.

"Good. Now, are we all okay with each other? I really can't stand all this friction, it isn't good for my health."

9 CONVERSATIONS

"I won't be at practice tonight," Anne said as they walked home from school Tuesday afternoon.

Alecia glanced at her friend, her eyes questioning. She waited for Anne to explain why, but no explanation came. "Is there a reason?" Alecia asked at last.

"Yeah, I have too much homework tonight and I have two tests at the end of the week. Good enough reason for you?" Anne snapped.

Alecia stared at her, amazed. Anne never snapped at people. "Take it easy, Annie," she said. "I was just asking."

"I'm sorry, Leesh. I'm feeling tired today," Anne apologized. "Will you tell Jeremy for me? I'll try to be there Thursday."

"Sure, I'll tell him. You'll be at the game this weekend though, won't you? It's a pretty big one, you know," Alecia reminded her.

Anne sighed and scuffed her shoe against the pavement. "We'll see," she said.

"Geez, Annie," Alecia said, glancing sideways at her

friend. "I'm beginning to think you don't like playing anymore."

"I don't know if I do, actually," Anne confessed. She looked up at Alecia, her face pale and anxious. "I haven't been sure for a while."

Alecia felt her heart sink and she swallowed hard. "Maybe if you take a day off and get some rest, you know, get this studying over with, you'll feel better?" she suggested hopefully but Anne looked doubtful.

"Maybe. Anyway," she went on, standing up straighter, "I'll see you tomorrow morning, right? Good luck with that math test you have to study for tonight," she said, forcing a smile.

Alecia watched her friend walk up her driveway and disappear into the house. She wished Connor had been with them. Connor was so much better at getting Anne out of her blue moods than Alecia was. Alecia could never think of the right thing to say. And he had to talk her out of quitting soccer! Alecia couldn't bear the thought of Anne not being at practices and games with her. Anne was the reason Alecia had stayed with the sport as long as she had. If Anne quit, what reason was there to continue?

★ ★ ★

"This is so much nicer than being outside!" Laurie Chen cried as she and Alecia practiced together. "Wasn't it awful Saturday? I don't like playing in the rain."

Alecia took a quick glance around the gym they were in. It was only an elementary school gym, the kind with the stage at one end and ropes hung from the ceiling, but it was a lot better than playing outside.

"Definitely," Alecia agreed, and concentrated on the complicated drill Jeremy had them doing. She dribbled the ball around the cones, then passed it to Laurie who was running alongside her. Laurie passed the ball back and Alecia had to trap it quickly, then continue running around the cones. She reached the end at last, and stopped to catch her breath. Laurie caught the ball and joined her.

"So, did you and Connor enjoy the movie?" she asked, leaning up against the wall.

"Yeah, it was okay. How 'bout you?"

"It was pretty funny. It was kind of corny in some places though."

"Connor said the same thing, actually," Alecia told her. The rest of the girls finished the drill and they lined up to go again, this time with Laurie dribbling around the cones and Alecia doing the passing.

"You and Connor have been friends for a long time, right?" Laurie continued, running the drill almost effortlessly.

"Quite a while, yeah," Alecia said, feeling a surge of jealousy at how good Laurie was at soccer.

"He's a nice guy. Friendly. You're lucky to have a

friend like that. A boy, I mean," Laurie said, trapping the ball.

"Most of the time, I guess," Alecia allowed, wondering what Laurie was getting at. She waited, but Laurie didn't say anything further. They finished the drill in silence, then found places to sit while Jeremy talked.

"We're going to give our goalkeepers a bit of a workout tonight, get them in shape for that big tournament coming up in a few weeks." Several of the girls shuddered at the mention of the tournament. The year before they had placed fifth out of eight, not a great showing. "Never mind the negativity. Let's divide into two groups and work at each net."

Alecia was always amazed at how good Stacie was in goal. She blocked almost every shot — leaping into the air to catch the high shots, diving and rolling to grab the low ones. Her hands were strong and confident and she never balked at the ball as it came hurtling toward her.

"How does she do it?" Alecia asked Nancy after Stacie just managed to catch Nancy's shot.

"Like I know," Nancy said, shaking her head. "I am so glad I play on her team, though."

Stacie was fearless, Alecia realized after half an hour of practice. It didn't matter to her that her knees and shins and elbows were permanently bruised and often a little torn up. Nor did she care that her hair was hanging in her eyes or that her gloves were soaked with perspiration. She continued to block almost all of the team's shots.

"I wish I could play with your enthusiasm, Stacie," Alecia said as they paused for a drink.

Stacie looked at Alecia, her gaze steady and thoughtful. "You could, Leesh, if you tried a little harder. I think you like soccer more than you let on." Stacie took another mouthful of water from her bottle and pushed the top down. She gave Alecia a friendly shove. "Just gotta work a little harder at it, Leesh, that's all," she said and headed back to her net.

Alecia was quiet on the short ride home, thinking about what Stacie had said, and about Anne. Anne's enthusiasm and love of the game were what kept Alecia going. She knew she needed the regular, intense exercise, and she actually didn't mind the running and passing. She enjoyed the time with the other girls, too. It was the wet and cold of the winter weather in Vancouver and the hard, stinging wet of the soccer ball when it pelted her in the legs or on her arms; the panting, smelly girls that ran into her and bodychecked her, interrupting good passes and shots on goal — those were the things she hated about soccer. How would she cope if Annie quit?

"You're pretty quiet tonight, Leesh," Jeremy said when they were almost home. He squeezed her shoulder gently. "Tough practice?"

"It was pretty good, I guess. Stacie sure is an

awesome goalkeeper," Alecia said, turning to face him in the dark car.

"Yes, she is. Do you know why?" Jeremy asked. "Because she puts in 150 per cent effort every single time we practise. She goes out on her own and practises too — I've seen her. Her brother shoots balls at her for hours sometimes."

"I don't have the time to do that," Alecia said, shaking her head.

"Of course you do, if you choose to make it. Stacie wants to play soccer. She wants to be the very best soccer player she can be and she is willing to work at it. Your heart isn't always in it. Sometimes — no, a lot of the time — I know you'd rather be out with Connor or sitting in front of the television."

Alecia smiled at how accurate Jeremy's picture of her was. He didn't say any of it as a criticism, he simply stated what was true. "Yeah, I know you're right. But what about Annie? She loves soccer, she convinced your couch potato daughter to take it up, and now she isn't sure she wants to keep playing. If she can change her mind about something she loves ... " Alecia paused, unsure what she was trying to say. She hadn't meant to tell Jeremy of Anne's doubts, but it was too late now.

"Anne does love soccer and she is a good, solid player. But sometimes other things come along in life that we discover we love even more than what we're already doing. I hope Anne doesn't quit soccer, but if she decides to, we're going to have to accept her decision, whether we like it or not," Jeremy said. He pulled into the garage and shut off the engine and the lights but neither of them made a move to get out of the car.

Alecia played with the strap of her bag. Part of her knew Jeremy was right but another little part hoped that if she tried hard enough, if she and Connor tried hard enough, they could convince Anne to stay with the team. Convince her that there was plenty of time for homework and friends and youth groups and church and even Tyler, as well as soccer. They could convince her, Alecia told herself as she slowly climbed out of the car. They *would* convince her.

10 ONE LESS PLAYER

Monica was waiting with Anne at their usual meeting spot on Wednesday morning. What's she doing here? Alecia wondered, catching Anne's eye, but Anne looked away. Alecia kept quiet, partly because it would have been rude to speak up in front of Monica, and partly because Monica started talking as soon as Connor and Alecia reached the two girls and never stopped, not once, until she had to go to her own locker in another hall.

"Hi! Isn't this marvellous? Annie and I have been waiting for you two to come along, just chatting and visiting. It's like we never see each other, really, although we do, all the time. And I was just telling Annie," she paused to flip her long hair out of her face, "how neat it would be if we could all get together sometime and get to know each other.

"I've been bowling with this league, it's pretty fun. I played in Toronto, and my mother insisted I had to do something. It's such a long, wet winter here in

Vancouver, isn't it? Positively sopping from October right through to April. So I was saying to Annie that you guys might like to go some time. It's fun, and drier than soccer, hey Annie?" Monica bumped against Anne, who giggled. "Of course, you have to find time between all the soccer practices you guys go to. Annie says you don't much like soccer, Alecia. You should try bowling, much drier — no sweat, so to speak."

"Do you do anything for exercise, Connor?" she asked and paused only briefly for him to say "Not really," before she continued on. "Annie said you were kind of a couch potato, like Alecia would be if she didn't play soccer," Monica said with a laugh and flipped her hair (for the fourth time in the last five minutes).

"Is this your locker already? I can't believe how quick the time goes when you're having a good time. I'll see you in gym, Annie, and you in band, Alecia. Ugh! We have that horrible Chopin thing to do today in front of the class! I completely forgot. See ya!"

She was gone. Alecia leaned against her locker and dropped her backpack, thoroughly exhausted.

"Whoa," Connor said through his teeth, watching Monica disappear around the corner. He grinned at Anne. "That is some mouth. She seems nice though, Annie," he allowed.

"She is!" Anne said, quickly, looking at Alecia as she spoke. "She is very caring and interested. She asks all sorts of questions about you guys, what we do together. She really wants to be friends with all of us."

"You certainly provide her with all the answers to her questions about us, too, eh Annie?" Alecia said, slamming her locker door open. She shoved her backpack inside and pulled out a handful of textbooks.

"Oh, well, I'm sorry if I told her too much. We just talk and talk. Sometimes I guess I tell her more than I should," Anne said.

"Never mind Annie," Connor said, patting her shoulder. "You only said what was the truth and besides, she may as well get an honest picture of us, right?" he asked.

Anne looked gratefully at him as she closed and locked her locker. "See you at lunch?" she asked, looking from Alecia to Connor.

"Yeah, see you at lunch," Alecia agreed.

"What have you got against Monica, Leesh?" Connor whispered as Anne walked away.

"The mouth, the hair flipping thing, the blabbing," she said.

Connor closed his locker and together they walked down the hall. "I think it's because Monica and Anne like each other and you feel threatened," he said.

"Do you stay up nights reading psychology textbooks?" Alecia asked. They had arrived at Alecia's class and stopped walking.

"Absolutely not. But I know you. Why don't you

give her a chance? Sure she talks way too much, but she's interesting, and yes she flips her hair, but you chew yours, and Anne and I put up with you anyway," Connor told her, bumping her shoulder as he spoke. Usually the shoulder bumping made Alecia smile, but today she only felt more annoyed.

"You don't know me at all, Connor Stevens. I'm not threatened by the Hair-Flipper and I don't chew my hair," she said as the bell rang. She slipped through the door before he could say anything else to annoy her further.

★ ★ ★

Alecia answered the phone that night when Anne called. "Hey, Annie, how's it going?" she asked, settling into a kitchen chair to talk. But Anne cleared her throat and asked for Jeremy. "Jeremy? Why do you want to talk to him?" Alecia asked, surprised. Then gradual realization spread through her. "You aren't phoning to quit the team, are you?" she cried.

"Could I please speak to Jeremy, Alecia?" Anne asked, shakily.

Alecia pulled herself out of her chair. "Certainly," she said. She handed the phone to Jeremy and left the room.

She was lying on her bed, facing the wall, when Jeremy knocked at the open door. "Can I come in?"

he asked and waited for her to roll over and nod before he came in and sat at the desk.

Alecia sat up and leaned against the pine headboard, pulling her knees in tightly to her chest. She rested her chin on her jeans and looked at Jeremy. "Annie quit the team," she said before he could say anything.

"Yes, Leesh, she did."

"Did she say why?" Alecia asked. She couldn't believe Anne had actually quit soccer. She could still hear her friend's arguments years ago, trying to convince Alecia to join with her. Had all those reasons been lies?

"Yes, she did tell me why. I think you'll have to ask her for her reasons yourself, though. I just wanted to make sure you would be okay with this," he said.

"No! I'm not okay with any of it!" Alecia cried, jumping from the bed to pace the room. "She's spent the last five years telling me what a great sport it is, how much fun running after a ball in the mud and cold is, what a great team we play for. Is that all a pack of lies now? Huh? She practically begged you to become our coach, even though I told her I didn't like the idea. She kept saying it would be great, all of it was always so great! And now, barely into the season, she changes her mind? Was all that other stuff lies?"

Jeremy let her talk herself out, then he reached out and took hold of her arms, pulling her close to him. Alecia let Jeremy hug her and felt some of her anger and frustration subside.

"Are you going to let her quit mid-season?" she said against his chest.

"Yes, I am. I don't want a player who doesn't want to be part of the team."

"Then I quit too," she said.

Jeremy pulled back from her and crossed his arms. "I beg your pardon?"

"I quit too. I only played because Anne was on the team. If she isn't on the team anymore, then neither am I."

"Are you listening to yourself, Alecia?" Jeremy asked. "I think you should think this over a bit. First of all, you are angry at Anne right now, and probably at me, too, for letting her leave. Second, you made a commitment to me, as well as the team, that you would play out this season. Third, your reasons for quitting are lousy." When Jeremy was particularly annoyed a little crease appeared between his eyes. It was there now. Alecia squirmed under it. She hated that crease.

"I don't want to play if Annie isn't on the team," she said, stubbornly, turning to stare at the floor.

"I have some work to do, and I'm sure you have homework for tomorrow. We can talk again later, but for now, the conversation is over," Jeremy told her and left the room.

Alecia didn't sleep well that night. In her dream she and Anne ran drills together in the pouring rain, wearing only shorts and their t-shirts. They started off close together, but as they ran, Anne got further and further away from Alecia, making it harder and harder to trap the ball and pass it back. She called to her friend, begging her to move closer so Alecia could make the passes, but Anne only got further away.

Alecia woke up at last, still tired and frustrated, both by the dream and by the reality. Anne would not be at practice that night, nor at the game on the weekend. She would never be at practices and games again. Alecia got angry all over just thinking about it and by the time she left for school an hour later, she was as angry as she had been the night before.

Connor was not at his spot and Alecia continued along alone to Anne's, not at all certain she wanted to talk to her. Anne was waiting, however, and fell into step beside Alecia on the sidewalk.

"Hi," she said softly, smiling rather hesitantly at Alecia.

"Hello. Jeremy told me you quit the team, but he wouldn't tell me why," Alecia said bluntly, concentrating hard on the stone she was moving along the sidewalk. Maybe, if she could keep the thing on the pavement all the way to the school, Annie would change her mind about quitting the team.

"Yeah, well," Anne began and paused. "The thing is, Leesh, it was getting too hard. So much homework all the time, two practices a week, and games most weekends. I'm really keen on ... on other things," she went on. "And my dad is concerned about my marks. He thinks maybe I have too much going on. He wants me to do well at school."

Alecia kicked her stone hard and watched as it went veering off the sidewalk and into the parking lot. "The team needs you," she muttered.

"Yeah, I guess. But I thought you'd understand, Leesh. I mean, you're my friend and everything," Anne said.

"I need you at practice, Annie! You're the only reason I play," she pleaded, hearing herself whine but not caring.

"You're a good player, Alecia," Anne told her. "You just need to stay focused when you're out there. I might come back next fall. Jeremy told me I could. Can't you please support my decision? I really want you to."

The bell rang and kids began moving past them toward the school. Alecia watched them for a minute, struggling. Then she saw the Hair-Flipper standing a little ways off, watching them, waiting for them to finish talking. Alecia stood up straighter. "I'll miss you, Annie," she said, deciding.

"Yeah, me too. I'll miss all of you," Anne said, with a grateful smile. "Thanks, Leesh." She squeezed Alecia's arm quickly then ran for the school. Alecia followed slowly behind.

11 FRIENDS DO THINGS LIKE THAT

"This is a pretty good photo, Leesh," Connor said. He was lying on his back on Alecia's bed, holding a photo of the soccer team above his head. He glanced over at Alecia, who was sitting at her desk.

"Not bad, I guess. Not that it matters, since they all end up in a drawer in a few days anyway," she said with a shrug. The pictures had been taken two weeks ago, before Anne had quit. Alecia sat beside Connor on the bed and looked at the photo over his shoulder. Alecia and Anne were side by side on one end of the bench. "Of course the picture is inaccurate now, isn't it? Not much point in keeping it," Alecia said, grabbing the photo from Connor and tossing it across the room.

"Hey! I was looking at that!" he said, jumping off the bed to retrieve it. "What is your problem? Are you still going on about Annie quitting?" he asked, returning to the bed. He flopped down again and went back to looking at the faces. "Because if that's it, get used to it, Leesh. She won't be coming back."

"No one asked you anything!" Alecia snapped. "I don't care what Anne Leung does! Don't think I do."

Connor looked at her silently for a while, no trace of a smile on his face. "*I* could join the team," he said at last, seriously.

Alecia laughed loudly at that, her anger slipping away. "You don't know the difference between a soccer ball and a baseball, Connor," she reminded him.

"I could learn, though, couldn't I?" he asked, still serious.

Alecia stopped laughing and sighed. She picked up the photo from the blue and yellow duvet and stared at all the faces, all the girls she had known for years: Stacie, Nancy, Allison, Rianne. Alecia and Anne had started playing with them when they were seven years old. Others had come and gone and there were some good players on the team now — nice girls, friendly, eager. But it wasn't going to be the same without Anne. "It isn't the same," Alecia whispered.

"Maybe you'll hit it off with some other girl now that Annie is gone," Connor suggested. "Laurie seems pretty nice."

Alecia shrugged. "They're all nice. Well, Nancy is a bit of a twit, she's still flirting with Jeremy. He told her to back off the other night at practice, she was being so ridiculous. Did I tell you Jeremy moved Allison Franklin into Anne's spot in forward?" she asked, touching Allison's face with her fingertip.

"Is that a good thing?"

"I guess we'll find out, won't we? He also named Laurie as team captain since Annie quit."

"Laurie? Really? That's pretty cool, right? I mean team captain is an important role, lots of responsibility and stuff?" Connor said, sitting up. He looked over at Alecia eagerly.

Alecia frowned at him. "Take it easy, Connor, it's not that exciting."

"Sure it is. I bet Laurie will do a great job, too, now that Annie is gone. She's been on the team a long time, hasn't she?" he asked, still with that annoying eager tone to his voice.

"Three years or so. What is *with* you?" Alecia asked, pushing him away from her and standing up. She moved across the room and stood by the window, her arms folded across her chest.

"Nothing. I'm just interested, that's all," he said. "Can't I be interested?"

"You've never asked so many questions about soccer. You hate soccer. And what's with all the questions about Laurie? What's going on there?" Alecia demanded.

Connor flushed and looked at the floor. "Nothing," he mumbled. "So what's with that history homework you needed help with?" he asked at last, going over to the desk. Alecia watched him silently for a second, debating whether to press the issue, then she decided against it and went over to find the work she was struggling with.

They worked quietly together for nearly an hour, talking only about the assignment Alecia was stuck on. At last they finished the outline and Alecia pushed it away from her. "Thanks. Now I can concentrate on the piles of other homework they keep throwing at me. Man, I hate high school," she said.

"It's not all bad, is it? I mean, there's the band, and lots of cute guys and all," Connor teased.

"What cute guys?" Alecia asked, lifting her head to look at her friend.

"Come on, you mean you never notice all the boys that stare at you? I see them when we walk down the hall together, watching you. I'm surprised you haven't had a dozen dates yet."

Alecia laughed too loudly and stood up. "You don't know how ridiculous you sound, Connor," she said awkwardly. "I'm only thirteen."

"And so? Anne's interested in that Tyler guy. You mean you aren't ... ?" he began, then glanced at her face and stopped speaking. "No, I guess you aren't," he finished under his breath. Alecia heard him, but had no desire to pursue the conversation.

"Well, maybe I should get going home," Connor decided, moving to the door. "I'll see you tomorrow, okay?"

"I'll be there. I was there today, and yesterday for that matter, same as always," Alecia told him. "You were the one who did a no-show."

"Yeah, well, I was busy," Connor said.

"Busy doing what?" Alecia asked as he pulled on his shoes at the front door. Through the doorway she could see her mother and Jeremy curled on the couch together, watching television. She turned her back on them. She hated it when they got all lovey-dovey newlywed-ish.

Connor tied his laces then stood up and looked at her for a second, frowning. "Alecia," he started. "Does, does Laurie ever talk about me at all?" he asked finally, his cheeks bright pink.

"Why would Laurie talk about you?" Alecia asked. "She doesn't even know you." She was lying to her best friend! Laurie asked about him all the time, pumping Alecia for information just as Connor was doing now.

"I don't know, but does she? Would you tell me?" The eagerness was back. It made Alecia feel squirmy. She wanted to slap it out of him.

"Why would I tell you? Huh? So you can go all dopey stupid in love over some girl?" she said meanly, trying desperately to disguise her discomfort.

"Friends do things like that for each other, Leesh," Connor said. "They help each other out sometimes. But maybe you wouldn't know anything about that." He opened the front door and stepped across the threshold. Alecia closed her eyes, felt her heart constrict, but held out her hand anyway, stopping him.

"Wait . . . " she said, and Connor stopped and turned around. "Laurie does ask about you. All the time," she confessed and wanted to cry at the happiness that appeared in Connor's face at her words.

"Really?" he said, his voice cracking. "Thanks Leesh, thanks a lot." He grinned at her, then turned, ran down the steps and disappeared into the shadowy November evening.

12 DEAD WEIGHT

Alecia tried again after dinner that evening to convince Jeremy to let her quit the team. She thought all her arguments out ahead of time, going through them carefully, trying to be rational but he only shook his head and said no.

"Look Alecia, I understand your feelings, I do. But you made a commitment and I expect you to honour it. You're reacting emotionally, not rationally right now and I'm not going to let you make decisions that way," he said in that annoying, calm way he had. He sat at the kitchen table and gazed at her, unruffled by her anger.

"Anne never made a rational decision. She was as emotional as they come and you accepted her decision without even arguing with her!" Alecia cried, recklessly slamming dishes into the washer.

"How do you know how I accepted her decision? You didn't hear the conversation. For all you know I made it very difficult for her. Look, I know you, and I know you think you can't cope without your friend being there. But you're wrong — you can. And if I see a lousy attitude and lack of effort, you'll regret it," he finished quietly, then left the room.

Alecia glared at him, but said nothing. Her mother, keeping to her promise to let them work things out themselves, kept quiet through the entire conversation, but Alecia thought she caught her smiling slightly to herself, which only upset Alecia more.

The car was a very silent place on the way to practice that night. Alecia pushed herself into a corner and stared sullenly out of the window. She was angry at Jeremy, but couldn't quite figure out what she was angriest about. Was it because he wouldn't let her quit or because he guessed she would try and sabotage herself and get herself kicked off the team? His tone of voice and the not-so-veiled threat had not been at all attractive, she decided. She much preferred the man who had dated her mother, the one who was so intent on Alecia liking him that he didn't dare step on her toes in any way. Those had been the days.

Alecia sighed. Her mother had warned her before the wedding last summer that once they all started living together there would be some adjusting to do. Alecia couldn't expect the dating Jeremy to be the same person as the daddy Jeremy.

"Do you remember those counselling sessions Mom dragged us to before the wedding?" Alecia asked suddenly, breaking the silence in the car.

Jeremy glanced at her, nodding. "I do. What about them?" he asked. He pulled into the parking lot of the school and came to a stop.

"They never covered playing soccer," Alecia said, and climbed out of the car.

Jeremy told the girls gathered in the middle of the gym floor that Anne wouldn't be returning that season for personal reasons. Although several of the girls asked, he refused to be more specific than that. Once they started their warm-up, however, Allison and Rianne appeared at Alecia's side.

"So why'd Annie quit, Leesh? She's one of the best players on the team," they said, jogging along slowly.

"She's just got a lot going on right now, that's all," Alecia told them. "She has a lot of homework and stuff."

"We all have homework and stuff," Allison pointed out. "There must have been more to it than that."

"Well, if there was," Alecia said, glancing at Allison and then back at the floor, "she hasn't told me about it."

Allison and Rianne shrugged and in another second moved away, leaving Alecia to run on her own. A couple of other girls came up alongside her to ask, but they were satisfied with a quick answer and she was alone when she came up behind Stacie and Nancy.

"I can't believe Annie quit," Alecia heard Nancy say. "I mean, she's one of the best players on the team, aside from being team captain."

"No kidding," Stacie agreed. "How come the dead

weight never quits, eh?" Alecia caught Nancy's eye as she glanced behind her. Nancy reddened and looked forward again, nudging Stacie with her elbow. In another second they had increased their pace and moved away. Behind them, Alecia stared at their retreating backs, her heart pounding. Did Stacie mean *her* when she said dead weight? Judging from Nancy's red face and little nudge, that was exactly who Stacie meant.

The idea bothered Alecia so much that she had trouble concentrating on the rest of the practice. She missed passes, passed poorly, nearly knocked Allison's head off with a poorly placed kick. She caught Jeremy watching her several times, but he said nothing to her. No one said anything to her, except for the occasional call of her name for a pass. Was it because she was dead weight? she wondered. Did they *all* wish it had been her who had quit rather than Anne? Everyone who asked about Anne said the same thing: She was such a good player, what a waste! Alecia was pretty sure no one would say things like that about her.

She was relieved when Jeremy called time and she could stop pretending to be interested. She headed off the floor toward the stage, where she had dumped her bag. Alecia idly scanned the crowd of parents waiting around the door, stopping when she got to a familiar face. She tossed her water bottle onto her bag and moved toward Connor, who was leaning against the back wall. She stopped suddenly, however, when she realized he wasn't waiting for her but for Laurie. Laurie had seen him and was by his side in a second. Alecia turned away and concentrated on gathering her things together and helping Jeremy clean up.

Connor and Laurie had disappeared when Alecia and Jeremy made their way out of the school and into the shadowy parking lot. She threw her bag in the back seat and opened her door, ready to climb in, when she saw movement by the gym wall. She squinted into the partial light given off by the streetlamp and recognized Laurie, leaning against the brick wall; standing very close to her, holding her hand, was Connor. Feeling as though she had seen something she shouldn't, Alecia jumped into the car and slammed her door shut, keeping her face turned deliberately away.

"Hey, isn't that Laurie and Connor by the gym?" Jeremy asked, pulling out of the parking lot.

Alecia looked at her stepfather, her eyes wide. "Where? I don't see anyone," she said.

"Over there, by the doors. I didn't know they were dating. I guess you guys are all getting older, I should expect that kind of thing. Should I get out my baseball bat?" Jeremy asked.

"What baseball bat?" Alecia asked, confused.

"The one they gave me when I became the father of a teenaged girl. You know, to keep the cute guys away from my beautiful daughter."

"Honestly, Jeremy, you don't know how ridiculous

you sound," Alecia snapped and leaned back in her seat, closing her eyes to try and lose the image of her best friend holding hands with a girl.

★ ★ ★

Anne phoned that night just after Alecia got home from practice. "How'd it go?" Anne asked once they had said hello.

"Oh, fine. Lots of people wondering why you quit though," Alecia told her, picking at the sandwich her mother had placed in front of her.

"What did you tell them?"

"I told them that you had a lot going on, that's all."

"Thanks Leesh. You have a game this weekend, eh?"

"Supposedly. I don't suppose you want to come and watch or anything?" Alecia asked. "Can you do that, even though you quit?"

"I can't come this weekend. There is a youth conference in Langley and I'm going to that. It's all weekend," Anne told her.

"Sounds like a blast," Alecia said sarcastically. "Will *Tyler* be there?"

"I don't know why you're being so nasty Alecia, but I don't like it. I think I'm going to hang up."

"Wait! Annie, I'm sorry, really. Don't hang up. It's just ... it was hard at practice without you. And no one wants me to be on the team and Jeremy won't let me quit," Alecia said, speaking quickly to prevent Anne from hanging up.

"What do you mean no one wants you to be on the team? That's ridiculous, Leesh. Who told you that?" Anne asked.

"I overheard Stacie tell Nancy she wished the dead weight would quit. I know she was talking about me. Everyone knows I only play because you're on the team." Alecia tossed the sandwich on the plate and pushed it away from her. She wiped at her eyes.

"Oh Alecia," Anne said and stopped.

"It's true! Why didn't you ever tell me, Annie?" Alecia asked. She felt betrayed.

"I did try, Alecia," Anne said softly and Alecia realized it was true. Anne had tried to tell her, Alecia had just ignored her. "The thing is, Leesh," Anne went on, "if you could adjust your thinking a little, you know, stop thinking of soccer as a chore, you might find you actually enjoy it. Maybe look on it as a challenge? See if you can change Stacie's mind about you. You are a good player, you just don't have much confidence," Anne told her.

"Thanks, Annie. I should go, I've got a ton of homework tonight. I'll see you in the morning, right? Just you, or will Monica be with you?" Alecia asked, doing her best not to sound nasty. Despite Anne's encouraging words, she still felt hurt that her teammates thought so poorly of her.

"Actually, Monica has a bad cold and won't be at school at all tomorrow," Anne told her. "So it'll be just the three of us."

"Well, I'll be there, anyway. I don't know about Connor, he has other interests," Alecia said, her voice barely hiding her dislike of the situation.

"Oh! I heard that Connor liked some girl but when I asked him about it he wouldn't tell me anything. Who is it?" Anne asked, her voice rising slightly.

"Laurie Chen," Alecia told her.

"No way! Laurie? That is too funny, don't you think? Does Laurie like him?" Anne asked, laughing.

"Apparently. They were holding hands outside the gym after practice tonight," Alecia told her, shuddering at the memory.

"Wow! Well, I guess it had to happen, right? I mean, he is a good-looking guy — girls are going to like him."

Alecia sat up in her chair and frowned at the wall. Connor, good-looking? she thought. "I really don't understand what all the fuss is with you and Connor about dating and stuff. Why can't we all just be friends like before?" she asked.

"Well, no one is asking me out on any dates. And besides, it isn't like they're getting married or anything, Leesh. They just like each other. It happens sometimes, you know," Anne said, laughing again. "See you tomorrow," she said and hung up.

Alecia sat for a long time, staring at the calendar

that hung by the phone. She had given her mother that calendar the previous Christmas. Every month had a different picture of a cow in some Vancouver scene or activity. At the time, Alecia had thought it was pretty funny. Now, it just looked stupid and idiotic and lame. Very, very lame.

13 FAMILY LIFE

Alecia finally stood up and wandered out of the kitchen. Her mother and Jeremy were reading in the living room. They looked up when she passed.

"Homework done yet, Leesh?" her mother asked, peering at Alecia over her reading glasses.

"I'm on my way," Alecia told her, continuing on up the stairs without stopping to chat.

She didn't have much to do, some history reading, some questions for English, and two pages of math problems. As she usually did, Alecia worked through everything else before finally picking up her math textbook and staring at the problems. She hated math with a passion. All semester she had been struggling with the work, staying in at lunch with the teacher to get a little extra help, barely passing tests, pulling out her hair over assignments. It didn't go any better tonight than it usually did.

Alecia battled the math for an hour until finally, completely frustrated and close to tears, she threw her pencil across the room. It made no sense to her. The numbers bounced around on the page infuriatingly, never doing what they were supposed to do.

"What possible use is it to know this stuff anyway!" she screamed at the posters on her wall. Aggravatingly, they didn't answer her. She wanted to gnash her teeth, tear at her hair, have a screaming, raging temper tantrum. She wanted to use every foul, unspeakable word ever invented.

"What is going on up here?" her mother asked, appearing at the door.

"I don't understand this stuff! I thought I did, but now I can't do it," Alecia said, throwing herself into her chair. Her mother came into the room, and glanced at the page of questions.

"Would you like some help?" she offered, not looking at her.

"Probably won't help anyway," Alecia mumbled, shrugging.

"Well, yelling at your walls isn't helping either, is it?" Mrs. Parker asked, maddeningly calm.

"NO! It isn't. But I don't know why you'd want to waste your time."

"Why don't you relax, and let's see if I can help you." Her mother read the first question to herself, and Alecia could tell by the expressions on her face that she was figuring it out in her head, then she read it out loud again, slowly.

"So, what's the first thing you have to do?" she asked when she finished reading. Alecia pointed to what she had written down on the paper but her mom frowned slightly and shook her head.

"No, not quite." She erased what Alecia had written and rewrote something completely different, talking as she did so. She put the pencil down when she got to the answer at the end and looked at her daughter. "See?" she asked.

Alecia didn't see, not at all. In fact she had understood more before her mother had tried to help her. "No. I don't see."

They tried another one, and another. But Alecia just got more and more confused and upset. Finally, she shoved the books away from her and slumped back in her chair.

"I don't *get* this! You're not helping!" she yelled. Mrs. Parker put down the pencil, looking slightly hurt.

"You have to try, Alecia. You can't just expect someone else to do it for you," she said, her voice tight.

"I *am* trying. I don't understand what you're saying," Alecia said, trying hard not to yell.

"How else can I explain it to you so you do understand?" her mom asked, running a hand across Alecia's head.

"What's going on up here?" Jeremy asked, appearing suddenly at the door. "You two trying to kill each other?"

"Alecia is having a tough time with her math homework and it seems I can't help her with it," Mrs. Parker explained. She stood up and rubbed a hand across her forehead, something she did when she was frustrated. She looked at Alecia one more time, but Alecia looked at her desk. She heard her mother going down the stairs and then it was quiet.

"What if I give it a try?" Jeremy asked, finally, picking up the textbook and reading it.

"It's a losing battle," Alecia said dejectedly. "You'd just be wasting your time."

"Let me be the judge of that," Jeremy said firmly. Alecia shrugged and showed him her notebook.

For an hour he went patiently over each question, trying to get her to see patterns to the questions. Sometimes she did see, and smiled happily as she worked the problem through to its end, but most of the time she nodded to everything he said, not understanding, not having a clue.

"You're not really getting this, are you?" he asked her once.

"Some of it, once in a while."

"That's what I thought. Have you always had this much trouble with math?" Jeremy asked.

"I can add and subtract, if that's what you mean," she said, rubbing her head.

"I meant with high school mathematics," Jeremy explained.

"I guess. But I've really only just started. I understood grade seven math. I hate being stupid at math, it's too stereotypical. You know, 'girls can't do math.' Thank God I'm good at science. Next semester, when I get science, I'll show all of you."

Jeremy laughed out loud, slammed the book shut and looked at her. "What would you say to my helping you on a regular basis?" he suggested, turning serious all of a sudden.

"Would you want to? Really? I mean, I can get a little violent," Alecia reminded him.

"I would like to help you if you will work at trying to understand."

"Thanks Jeremy, I'd like that," she said.

"We all run up against things we think will defeat us. The trick is to stare them down. Can I tell you a secret?" he whispered and she nodded. "I can't spell worth beans, never could. My teachers used to give my papers back so crossed out with red pen, you couldn't read the work. I mean, I couldn't even spell 'it' right half the time."

"You keep helping me with math and I'll tutor you in spelling," Alecia said, smiling.

"Deal," Jeremy agreed, then turned to leave the room.

"Hey," she said. He stopped and looked at her again. "You spell 'it' I-T." He smacked her arm, laughing, as he left the room.

14 THE TRUTH HURTS

Monica had recovered by Monday morning and was waiting with Anne when Connor and Alecia arrived just after eight. She was still coughing and sneezing and Alecia put both Anne and Connor between them.

"Don't worry Alecia, I'm not contagious anymore. Mom says colds are only contagious in the first few days, not at the end. I never knew that, did you?" Monica asked, but didn't wait for an answer. "Annie and I were just reliving that youth conference we went to this weekend. It was so fun! There was a dance Saturday night and Tyler asked Anne to dance! Three times! I keep trying to tell her he likes her, but she won't believe me. Maybe Alecia can convince you, eh Alecia? You know he likes her, help me convince Annie here."

Alecia looked briefly at Monica then faced forward again. "Anne is too young for a boyfriend, her father would never let her go out with him even if he does like her," she said, primly. She felt Connor's elbow in her ribs but ignored him.

"Oh, I don't believe that! Thirteen is not too young. How old were you when you went on your first date, Connor?" Monica asked, flipping her hair from her face.

Connor blushed and looked at the ground, clearing his throat several times before he managed to speak. "Well, actually," he began and paused as all three girls stopped walking to look at him. "I guess fourteen."

"You're going out with Laurie, aren't you?" Anne asked, grinning at him. "That is so cool, Connor!"

Alecia said nothing as the other two girls pummelled him and asked him questions. She couldn't tell if he was enjoying their attention or regretting having said anything. She didn't really care. He could have told her privately. They *were* supposed to be best friends.

"I was going to tell you last night, Leesh," Connor whispered in her ear once they'd all resumed walking, "but the line was busy when I called and I never got near the phone again. I'm sorry. Are you mad?" he asked, holding her arm tightly.

"Of course not. You can do what you want, right? Free world and everything," she said, thinking of him and Laurie standing outside the school gym. She blinked and smiled somewhat stiffly. "I hope you have a good time."

"Oh you will!" Monica said, almost dancing on the sidewalk. "This Friday, is that when you're going out? Well I guess you won't be able to join us on our bowling outing then," she went on, pausing only long enough to let Connor respond to her question. "Annie and I have been planning it all out. Bowling at the lanes, then pizza afterward. Doesn't that sound like a blast?"

"You'll come won't you, Leesh?" Anne asked, leaning in close to Alecia.

"I don't like bowling, Annie," she said. They had made it to the high school and were immediately surrounded by hundreds of students all trying to get through a limited number of doors. Alecia frowned as she was bumped and stepped on. Connor disappeared almost immediately; probably in search of Laurie, Alecia decided.

"You've never even been, Leesh," Anne reminded her. "Come with us, please? It will be fun. And you love pizza," she added.

"You have to come, Alecia," Monica added as they pushed their way through the doors. "We need a foursome. As it is, without Connor we might have to ask *Tyler*."

"I do not have to come," Alecia said, her voice taking on an edge. "I do not want to go bowling with you or eat pizza either, for that matter." She looked directly at Monica as she spoke, making sure the girl understood her meaning. Monica did. She flushed and looked down the hall.

"Well, I guess I should get to my locker! Don't want to be late, eh?" she said — too brightly — and disappeared.

Anne glared at Alecia. "I can't believe how rude you can be, Alecia," she said and turned away.

"She is so pushy, Annie!" Alecia defended herself. "I told you both that I didn't want to go bowling and she wouldn't leave it alone. I really don't see what you like about her."

"You told her you didn't want to go with *her*. Even I got that message! You hurt her feelings, Alecia. I can't believe you did that," Anne said. "And I'll tell you why I like her. She encourages me and supports my decisions and makes me feel good about myself! She doesn't order me around and expect me to do what she wants to do all the time. She's willing to try new things and meet new people, and she accepts people for who they are without judging them."

Alecia's surprise showed on her face. She felt as though she had been slapped. "Well," she said, at a loss for words. "I didn't realize I was such a lousy, miserable friend."

"Look, Alecia, you're not a lousy friend. It's just... why can't I be friends with both of you?" Anne asked, her anger subsiding.

"I'm not forcing you to choose between us, Annie," Alecia said.

"Yes, Alecia, you are," Anne said quietly and closed her locker before walking away to her homeroom.

Alecia found herself walking home alone that afternoon, feeling miserable. The week had started out lousy and just got worse. First Stacie had called her dead weight at soccer and now she'd had an argument with Annie. Alecia was angry and upset and lonely. She had seen Connor walking off with Laurie in another direction and Anne was with Monica somewhere. Every stone that crossed her path felt the brunt of her frustrated anger on that walk home but there weren't enough to diffuse it. She arrived at her empty house just as angry as when she had left the school.

She was watching a talk show when her mother came home from work just after five. Alecia had done no homework, hadn't started dinner, hadn't straightened her room or put away her things from school. Her mother stood in the doorway and folded her arms across her chest. Alecia knew she hated coming home to a mess and a sullen, miserable daughter, but Alecia didn't care.

"Obviously, something is wrong," Mrs. Parker said. "Perhaps you'll be so kind as to fill me in before I start yelling at you for lying around, neglecting your responsibilities."

"Life is —!" Alecia cried, jumping off the couch to pace the family room.

"Don't speak that way, if you don't mind. I don't care how mad you are. Calm yourself and tell me what has happened," her mother said evenly.

Alecia stormed around the room for another minute or two, feeling like a caged animal. Finally, however, she told her mother everything that had happened, starting with Stacie calling her dead weight and ending with all the nasty, unkind words that had been spoken by her and Anne, all the hurt looks and surprise announcements. When she was finished she felt drained and sank into Jeremy's big leather easy chair. "I don't understand why everyone is acting this way," she said, calmer now. "Stacie is being so mean to me and Annie acts like I've stabbed her in the heart or something."

Her mother moved from her spot by the door over to the couch and sat down. She smoothed her skirt over her knees and cleared her throat. "Alecia, did you stop to think about the things people have said to you?" she asked, speaking slowly, deliberately.

"You mean about how I'm a dead weight on the team and what a lousy, miserable friend I am? No, they just said those things to hurt me," Alecia said.

"Anne didn't say you were a miserable friend, Alecia. You're the one saying that. But maybe you need to think about what Annie did say, and what Stacie said; hear their words. Are they true? Are you like that?"

Was she? Alecia forced herself to think about Stacie's words and Anne's. Did she tell Anne what to do, expect her to do what Alecia wanted, criticize her choices? Was she dead weight on the team? If she was honest with herself, she had to admit the answer to both questions was yes. "I do all those things! But I don't mean to, Mom," she whispered, tears swelling in her eyes. She brushed them away and sniffed.

"Oh Alecia, I'm sure you don't," Mrs. Parker said gently. "But obviously you have been and Anne is tired of it. She doesn't want to be told who to be friends with and who not to be friends with. And it isn't fair of you to force her to choose."

"I'm not making her choose between us!" Alecia objected. "I just don't want to be friends with the Hair-Flipper. Sorry," she said, catching her mother's look, "Monica. I don't like her."

"You force her to make a choice between you when you won't accept that she and Monica are friends, and when you won't at least try to get to know her. You force her to make a choice when you bad-mouth Monica, when you call her the Hair-Flipper." She pulled Alecia close to her and held her tightly, brushing the loose hairs from her face.

"Why is everything so complicated? Why can't Connor and Anne just be the way they always were?" Alecia whispered into her mother's suit jacket.

"Because if people don't change, don't grow, then they die inside," her mother told her. "I don't mean literally die, obviously, but their souls just kind of stagnate. Would you really want to stay thirteen for the rest of your life? Of course not. But you can't age in years without aging in other ways as well. Connor liking Laurie, Anne going to church, those are their ways of exploring their worlds, of growing."

"I feel like I'm being left behind," Alecia confessed. "No one is waiting for me to change too. Why don't I like boys? Why don't I want to go to church and belong to a youth group and try bowling and make new friends?" she asked, sitting away from her mother.

"We all change at our own speed. There are no rules for people to follow. When you're ready you will like boys, want to date them. The thing is, sweetie, you can't force things on yourself and you definitely can't force things on other people. The more you try and control Connor and Anne, the more they are going to go in their own directions. And you will be left with neither of them."

"I really hate being thirteen, Mom," Alecia said, sighing heavily.

"I know. But we'll all survive it, and you know what? You'll be fourteen in a few more months," her mother reminded her, but Alecia only grunted. Her mother reached up and undid the clasp holding her hair back. She sighed happily as it fell down around her shoulders. "That feels much better," she said, leaning back against the cushions.

"What about Stacie?" Alecia asked awhile later, looking up at her mother. "Maybe I should just quit the team, make everyone happy."

"Quitting doesn't really solve the problem," Mrs. Parker said.

"But I only play because Annie plays," Alecia whined.

"That is not true. You might have started playing because Anne was joining, but you haven't stayed with it all these years for that reason. You just don't want to believe you actually like the game. Come on, Leesh, take a good hard look at yourself and your reasons for playing. Stop hiding behind your old excuses," her mother told her firmly.

Alecia looked at her mother, frowning. Why did she continue playing soccer? she wondered. It had become a kind of habit for Alecia to whine about playing. It was what she did. Nancy flirted, Laurie kept peace among the players, and Alecia whined. But suddenly she realized that she didn't mean it. It was just that, a bad habit. Sometimes, Alecia acknowledged to herself, she whined automatically and not because she actually meant what she said. She hated playing games in the pouring rain and cold, but she enjoyed practising and trying new skills.

"I guess I play because I like the challenge," she said, amazed at her own words. "Because I like the other girls and being part of the team."

"Don't look so surprised!" Mrs. Parker said, giving Alecia a little push. "Those are excellent reasons to play. Now what are you going to do about Stacie?"

"Prove her wrong," Alecia said firmly.

15 TOURNAMENT TIME

"What has happened to you lately, Leesh?" Laurie asked as they paused for water during Thursday's practice the following week.

"What do you mean?" Alecia asked, suddenly nervous that she had done something wrong, been "dead weight" again.

"You are playing like a demon," Laurie told her, shaking her head. She took another mouthful of water and capped her bottle. "I've been watching you. You're really into it all of a sudden, making plays, tackling hard, fighting to keep the ball. I'm impressed." Laurie grinned at her and then headed back to the floor.

Alecia stared after her, grinning too. Ever since her talk with her mother, Alecia had been trying hard. Each practice she had challenged herself to focus on one thing and work at it. It felt great to know that the team's captain had noticed. She worked with renewed energy and determination after that and, on the ride home, discovered that someone else had noticed her efforts.

"You've been playing better than I've ever seen you play, Leesh," Jeremy told her, as they drove home that night.

"Really?" Alecia asked.

"Really. You've been involved and focused. And it looks as though you're enjoying yourself, getting something out of the practice. I'm glad to see you having a good time out there, Leesh. Soccer is a great game and you have skill."

Alecia rolled her eyes at Jeremy, embarrassed by his words. "Watch it, or all this praise will give me a fat head," she warned. Still, as she stared out the window, she felt a warm glow spread through her.

★ ★ ★

"Doesn't it just figure?" Stacie grumbled Saturday morning as they gathered for their first game of the tournament. "Doesn't it just figure that it would be this weekend that three people are sick? What are they thinking?"

Nancy and Rianne, busy tying their cleats nearby, giggled and shook their heads at Stacie's grumblings. "Come on Stace, this always happens!" Rianne reminded her. "Remember last year? You, Laurie, and Allison were all sicker than dogs." Rianne shrugged. "It happens."

"People should have more commitment to the

team. This is an important tournament," Stacie went on, adjusting her pads.

It *was* an important tournament. The community league the Burrards played in had only a few tournaments a year and often the winner of the first one went on to win the last one as well. Last year the Burrards had bombed big time — partially, Alecia realized, because of all the sickness, but also because they weren't playing as a team. Alecia knew they were playing much better this year and told Stacie so.

"According to who?" Stacie demanded, putting her hands on her hips and glaring at Alecia. Alecia looked at her steadily.

"Jeremy, that's who," she told her, smugly.

"Well, maybe," Stacie allowed. "But these teams are just as good and they appear to be all healthy."

"We play the Crusaders first and they are not the greatest team in the league," Allison said, joining them at the bench. "In fact, their regular goalkeeper is benched with a sprained ankle, so we have an excellent chance of beating them. Win the first, the next is easier, right?"

"You don't have to convince me, Stacie is the one doing all the grumbling," Alecia said, grinning as Stacie scowled at her.

"Quit your grumbling and let's get on with this thing. I have a date tonight!" Allison called, grabbing a ball and running onto the field.

Laurie waved to Alecia and Alecia joined her to

warm up. "How's it going?" Laurie asked as they passed a ball between them.

"Not bad. I hope we don't get creamed this weekend."

"We could really use Annie," Laurie said, trapping Alecia's pass and sending it back.

"Yeah, well, she said she was coming to watch. Maybe you can convince her to play a couple of shifts," Alecia said.

"You and Annie okay these days?" Laurie asked.

"Not really," Alecia confessed, giving the ball a vicious kick.

"That's crappy. I know what it's like though," Laurie told her. "Last year, my best friend, Taylor, got all involved in drama classes and turned into this really stuck-up person, always acting so important because she had a part in the school play! Anyway, she thought I should give up soccer, try something more feminine, wear a skirt once in a while. I got tired of it, told her where to go, and life has been much smoother since. Sometimes you just go in different directions, you know? No one's fault or anything. You just start wanting different things, seeing the world differently." Laurie laughed and picked up the soccer ball. "At least that's the line my mother fed me when I was coming home from school every day crying or throwing things."

Alecia laughed at that, hearing her own mother's endless stream of wisdom in her ears. "Yeah, mine has lots of advice too," she said. "Help me stretch out my neck, will you? If I don't learn how to head that ball soon I'm going to kill myself."

They won their first game 2–1, as Allison had predicted, but not without a fight. The Crusaders might have had an inexperienced goalkeeper, but their defence was watching out for her. Every play the Burrards made there appeared to be five or six large Crusader defenders right there, blocking and tackling.

"That was tough," someone muttered as they left the field at the final whistle.

"Yeah, but not as tough as the next game will be. I just heard that the Rocketeers won their first game too, so we'll be playing them," Stacie told them and everyone groaned.

"Go in with an attitude like that and you will lose," Jeremy told them firmly. "We've talked about the Rocketeers' game and what to watch for. You can play this game and win it if you concentrate and stay focused."

In the break between games, the girls lay around on the grass, talking, eating oranges, discussing the play, eyeing the spectators, and resting. Mrs. Parker showed up with Alecia's grandparents just before the Burrards' second game started, followed shortly by Anne and Connor. Alecia noticed all of them, but made no effort to say hello, except for a quick wave in their general direction. Her nerves were shot and she wanted only to concentrate on the game. She didn't want to be distracted by anything.

Laurie won the toss and got the kick for the start of their second game, against the Rocketeers. They were all nervous, despite Jeremy's encouragement. Laurie's first pass, a weak shot to Allison on her right, was stolen by a powerful forward from the other team. The girl barrelled back across the centre line and chipped the ball away just as Alecia stuck her foot out to steal it. Nancy caught it and kicked it to Laurie at the centre line. Laurie carried the ball up the middle. On both sides of her, moving in quickly, were Rocketeer forwards. To Alecia, standing just over the centre line, they looked like locomotives, not girls. In another second Laurie would be mowed down.

"Pass!" Alecia screamed just before Laurie was tackled. Alecia caught the frantic pass, steadied it, and looked around quickly for backup. There seemed to be many more Rocketeers on the field than Burrards, and for a second Alecia couldn't see any familiar purple jerseys. She kept the ball in tight and made her way down the field toward the Rocketeers' net, her eyes scanning for an open player.

A huge Rocketeer defender appeared out of nowhere in front of her, blocking out the entire field. Alecia turned, keeping her body between the girl and the ball, and found herself out of bounds. The referee blew the whistle and the Rocketeer centre grabbed the ball for a throw-in.

"Feeling a bit of pressure?" The Rocketeers' centre taunted as she moved past Alecia. Alecia stuck out her tongue. The girl was known for her mouthiness.

"You might be bigger than us, but we have way more style," Allison shot back, winking at Alecia. They jostled for position as the girl drew the ball over her head and lobbed it out onto the field. It came down in a perfect arc and was met by Nancy and a Rocketeer forward. Alecia watched carefully, prepared to take Nancy's pass if she got possession. The two girls jumped toward the ball at the same time and as they came down the Rocketeer stuck out her foot and caught Nancy's ankle, sending her rolling to the ground. Alecia called out, but the referee hadn't seen it and no foul was called.

Furious, Alecia tore after the Rocketeer who had picked up the ball and was moving quickly toward Stacie. Alecia caught up to the forward and challenged her hard for the ball. Every time the girl moved right, Alecia moved right. If she faked right and went left, Alecia went left too. All those years of playing with Annie had paid off. She could be as annoying as anyone. Finally, frustrated and unable to get a shot away, the Rocketeer shoved Alecia, sending her flying to the ground. She landed hard on her rear as the referee blew the whistle.

"Thanks, Alecia," Nancy whispered as they passed each other. "I didn't think anyone had seen."

"She won't try and get away with that again," Alecia

said firmly, rubbing her rear end.

She stood patiently outside the penalty crease for the free kick, waiting for her teammates to get in position. Alecia couldn't kick directly on goal but Laurie could and she and Alecia made quick eye contact just as Alecia sent the ball flying through the air toward her. It came down only a couple of feet away from Laurie and she was on top of it immediately. Just as quickly she shot the ball at the net. She had aimed for the upper right-hand corner and that was exactly where it went, falling to the ground just over the goal line and out of reach of the Rocketeers' goalkeeper. The Burrards cheered and Laurie was mobbed from all sides by purple jerseys. Their captain looked around rather sheepishly.

"One–nothing! Way to go Laurie! Way to go Alecia!" the girls cried, pounding them both on the back.

"How's that for justice?" Nancy said to Alecia as they headed back to centre for the faceoff. Alecia grinned. Her bruised backside and Nancy's sore ankle were a small price to pay for scoring the first goal of the game, she decided.

The Burrards kept working hard but, with the goal, the Rocketeers became even more pushy and aggressive. Alecia and her teammates found themselves spending most of their time defending their goal and very little time creating offensive play. One after another the Rocketeers bolted up the middle, charging through the Burrard defence as though it wasn't there. Again and again they shot on Stacie, sending her flying left and right to catch the ball. Soon Stacie was covered in mud and grass, a large purple welt growing on her thigh.

"What the heck is going on?" Allison asked as they grouped for a throw-in.

"They're killing us, that's what is going on," Alecia grumbled, rubbing the spot on her leg that had connected with the ball in the last play.

"You guys ready to give up yet?" the Rocketeers' centre taunted, grinning at them.

"Why should we give up?" Nancy called back, her face and neck red with frustration and effort. "We're still winning, in case you hadn't noticed!"

The ball was thrown in just to the left of Stacie. A Rocketeer forward trapped it with her chest, then quickly got control of it on the ground, moving effortlessly around Alecia's block and then Nancy's. She passed the ball back to the centre line, away from the traffic set up by the Burrards, while the Rocketeer centre received it and dribbled back toward the net. Gradually she increased her speed until she was running full out. Rianne ran to block her, challenging her hard, but suddenly the ball was gone, kicked through her legs. Rianne looked frantically around for a second, trying to figure out what had happened, but by the time she found it, the ball had been picked up by a strong forward. The forward broke free of Nancy and Alecia and headed for the net.

Her shot was hard and true and Stacie only just managed to tip it away. The Rocketeer centre had moved right up on the play, however, and was there, waiting for the rebound. Allison threw herself at the girl, pushing her off her stride and almost making her trip, but she stayed upright and in another second had gained the net again. This time the ball went in. The Burrards groaned, cringing at the Rocketeers' loud whoops and cheers. Now it was tied!

"Come on you guys," Laurie hissed as they headed back to centre for another faceoff. She clapped her hands, encouraging them. "Keep it together. Only five minutes to halftime and we can rest. Until then, keep fighting! We can't let these Clydesdales beat us!"

Clydesdales! Alecia had called this team Clydesdales the night Laurie and Connor met at the movies. She sighed heavily as she took up her position on the field. She had seen Laurie look for Connor on the sidelines after her goal, had seen the grin he gave her. It made Alecia feel funny inside, funny and lonely, as though she had lost someone. She shook her head and turned away from the sidelines and back to the game. She had to concentrate hard. There wasn't time to think about Laurie and Connor.

16 HEADS UP!

Laurie's little pep talk helped and the Burrards held on to finish the first half in a tie. They were exhausted, and a number of the girls collapsed to the grass around the bench, groaning as they closed their eyes. Mrs. Parker handed out oranges, water bottles appeared from bags, and gradually energy returned to the team. They listened carefully to Jeremy's instructions.

"You played well. There were some solid plays out there and some good defence. They are a big team and strong, but you girls are quick and agile. Remember what we've discussed. Don't let them intimidate you. Alecia, that play on the forward who tripped Nancy was excellent. You wore her out, made her mess up. It pays to be annoying. You can't be bigger or stronger than they are but you can use your smaller size to your advantage. Be in their faces, annoy them, get them to make the mistakes." The whistle blew and water bottles were tossed aside as they made their way back onto the field.

The Rocketeers won the toss and started the game with a series of short running passes. The centre kicked it to a forward who passed it back to the centre who turned, abruptly, and headed back toward her own end. Confused, the Burrards scrambled, trying to get back over the centre line. But the girl had already turned again and was running straight up the middle toward Stacie. Stacie moved out of her net, making herself larger. She bounced on the balls of her feet and had her gloved hands up in front of her, ready to catch anything the opposition might send her.

Just as the Rocketeer got set to kick, Nancy appeared and slid into her, knocking the ball just far enough away that Laurie could get it and send it flying up the field.

"Good play, Nance," Alecia called as she ran past.

"Thanks Leesh," Nancy muttered, rubbing her grass-stained leg.

Despite several good chances on both sides, the score remained tied at one apiece until late in the second half. Jeremy started rotating players a bit more often, giving everyone a chance to rest. Alecia was reluctant to leave the game when Rianne tapped her on the shoulder and pointed at the bench during a stop in play, but she ran off anyway and found a seat. She took several deep swallows from her water bottle and stretched out her legs as she watched from the sidelines. When Jeremy motioned for her to return to the field, Alecia realized the short rest had helped. She had renewed energy.

Almost as soon as the ball was thrown into play after the foul, Laurie, Nancy, and Rianne became involved in a skirmish near Stacie. As they desperately tried to block three big Rocketeer forwards from taking a shot, Alecia moved into a space just beyond the play and raised her arm. Laurie saw her and passed her the ball. Meeting the ball in mid-stride, Alecia picked it up and dribbled out of the Burrards' end and back toward the Rocketeer goal. She kept an eye on the rest of the players and was aware that a very large defender was making her way toward her. Alecia stepped to one side, faking a pass, then turned and passed the ball to Allison, who was waiting near the goal. Allison was immediately tackled from behind and quickly sent the ball back to Alecia. Alecia saw it coming at her, arcing through the air in a perfect curve, and realized she would have to head it.

She stiffened the muscles in her neck, moved beneath the falling ball, then leaned back, and, never taking her eyes from the ball, snapped her body forward as the ball hit her square in the forehead. It was a clean, centred connection and the ball flew in the direction of the net and was kicked into the goal by Allison, who was waiting for it.

The Burrards erupted into screams and suddenly there were what seemed like dozens of bodies hugging Alecia and Allison. They jumped up and down in unison for several seconds before breaking apart and returning to their kickoff positions. The last ten minutes of the game went by quickly. The Rocketeers tried hard, but they couldn't get through the line of defenders the Burrards set up in front of Stacie and in the end, Allison's goal won them the game.

"This is not the end of it, ladies," Jeremy reminded them as they came off the field, clapping each other on the back and whooping. "There are more games to be played." He looked around at the excited faces, caught Alecia's eye, and shook his head, laughing. "Aww, to heck with it! That was a very solid, well-played game. You should be proud of yourselves," he admitted, allowing himself to lose his cool facade. "You did a great job, Alecia." Jeremy said, smiling at her. She could see the pride in his eyes and felt herself blush slightly.

"I'm starving!" she cried, embarrassed, and broke from the crowd of people. She grabbed her team jacket, slipping it on against the chill of the November day, and went in search of her mother, who had promised to bring lunch.

The crowd had broken up slightly but Alecia couldn't see her mother anywhere. She wandered around aimlessly for a few minutes, scanning the people, and nearly bumped right into Anne. They looked at each other for a long minute before Anne finally broke the silence.

"That was some game, Alecia. You played very well," Anne said, politely.

"Thank you. We're doing okay, I guess."

"If you win your next game you'll be undefeated, get a good position for the finals. That would be awesome," Anne pointed out.

They stood awkwardly, looking at each other. Alecia had never felt so uncomfortable around Anne before. "Where's *Monica* today?" she asked, regretting the words as soon as they were spoken. Why had she brought up her name? she asked herself.

"Why are you being like this, Alecia? I don't understand," Anne said, hurt.

"*I'm* not being like anything," Alecia said stiffly. "*You're* the one who's insisting I be friends with Monica."

"I'm not insisting you be anything. I just don't think it's fair of you to make me choose between you or Monica. Why can't I be friends with both of you?"

Alecia thought of her mother's words, of their conversation from the other day. Suddenly Alecia realized that Monica wasn't the problem, had never been the problem.

"You're different, Annie. You've changed," she said, her voice low.

"I'm no different," Anne argued, looking surprised.

"Yes you are. You go to church, you go to some youth group thing, you're never around on the weekends, you want to try bowling and babysitting and stuff. You aren't interested in soccer anymore." Anne looked at her, frowning, but said nothing. "We're not interested in the same things. You want to do things I don't want to do and you like boys now, and are meeting new friends. I'm just the same."

"You're changing too, Leesh, just not in the same ways. You played an awesome game of soccer and I can tell you are really enjoying it now. That's new, right?" Anne asked. "Everyone is changing, Leesh. It happens." Anne lifted her hand as she spoke, as though she were reaching for Alecia, then dropped it. Alecia swallowed hard, trying not to cry. She *would not* cry, she told herself sternly, not here in front of her teammates. Her mother appeared, just beyond Anne, carrying a huge picnic basket. Alecia blinked several times, quickly, trying to clear the tears from her eyes.

"Yeah, well, I guess I should go help my mom," she said. "I'll see you around." She cleared her throat again and moved away, leaving Anne standing alone.

17 A NEW OUTLOOK ON THINGS

The tournament went on all the rest of Saturday and finished Sunday afternoon. Alecia and her parents arrived home at dinnertime Sunday tired, dirty, and triumphant.

"SECOND!" Alecia called through the door as they came in the house. "Can you believe that? We only lost one game the whole weekend!" she cried, dropping gear and clothing in piles as she moved into the kitchen. "What a tournament! What a difference from last year!" Her mother smiled at her and shook her head.

"What?" Alecia demanded, so pumped she couldn't stop moving.

"Nothing," Mrs. Parker said, still smiling. "It's just I've never seen you so excited about soccer before. It's wonderful."

Alecia ignored her mother's comment. "And we creamed the Rocketeers. They came in fifth! And we would have had first place wrapped up if it hadn't been for that penalty shot." She sighed, thinking of their last game and the unfortunate penalty Nancy had received in the last five minutes. They had lost 2–1. In the end, though, no one really cared. It had been a great weekend.

"You girls did an awesome job all weekend. I am immensely proud of you, all of you," Jeremy said quietly, pulling out a chair and dropping down. He looked worn out.

Alecia stopped prancing around the kitchen and walked over to her stepfather. She stood in front of him, still wearing her dirty shorts and grass-covered jersey. Her braid was coming loose and curls of hair floated around her face. She desperately needed a shower and a hot meal and a long, long sleep. But first she had something to say and she had to say it now.

"I wanted to say thank you, Jeremy," Alecia began slowly, her voice soft. "Thank you for taking on our team this season and thank you for not letting me quit." She leaned over and kissed his cheek quickly, then turned and ran from the room, leaving Jeremy sitting speechless behind her.

★ ★ ★

November finally ended and December rolled in. The days were a little less wet and the air was crisp and clean. There weren't many soccer games scheduled for December, as school wound down for the holidays, and Alecia found herself missing them. She had never thought she would actually miss playing, but she did. The weekends seemed long without a game. The weekends seemed long without Anne, too, Alecia admitted reluctantly to herself. She missed Anne so much it hurt, all the time, but she didn't know what to do to fix the problem.

She missed Connor too, but in a different way. They saw each other, but Laurie was usually with them. It seemed the days of laying around talking and playing video games were over. She missed their inside jokes and teasing. She missed the last-minute Friday night movies and long phone calls that only ended when one of their parents or Connor's older sister yelled at them to get off the phone. She missed his help with her homework. Surprisingly, Alecia even missed the nagging and lectures.

Then, one Saturday afternoon when there was no game, Laurie and Connor arrived at the door. "Wanna go kick the ball around?" Laurie asked, showing Alecia the soccer ball she carried. Beside her, Connor shook his head.

"I tried to talk her out of it, Leesh," he said, raising his hands in defeat. "But she wouldn't listen. I told her you hated soccer and would never practise just for the heck of it." Alecia was ready to object, to defend herself against his words when she caught the twinkle in his blue eyes and the wink he sent to Laurie. She laughed instead.

"I was just wondering what to do with myself," she said. "This sounds better than anything I was coming up with. Just let me get my shoes on and grab a sweatshirt. Did you want to come in and wait?" she asked, holding the door open.

"Connor would have stayed in all afternoon playing video games if I hadn't come along and rescued him," Laurie said as they headed down the sidewalk together five minutes later.

"Hey!" Connor cried. "I didn't need rescuing! I was perfectly happy sitting on my favourite bean bag chair in front of the TV."

"Laurie, I've been trying to get Connor off the couch for years," Alecia said, shaking her head sadly. "He is the world's laziest human being."

"I'll have you know, Miss Alecia Smarty-Pants, that I am a reformed man. I have cut my gaming down to a mere two hours a day since I met Laurie. So there."

Alecia looked at the two of them and smiled. It was nice to see her best friend so happy. He obviously liked Laurie a lot and from the look on Laurie's face, she felt the same. Alecia was happy for them. The awful, hurting jealousy she had been feeling for weeks had slipped quietly away and she didn't even cringe when Connor reached for Laurie's hand and held it the rest of the way to the playing field.

The field was empty when they arrived. Connor dropped to the bench. "I'll be coach and yell at you both from here," he said, getting comfortable.

"You'll get lots of exercise doing that," Alecia told him, laughing as Laurie kicked at his shins.

"Okay, okay!" Connor cried, jumping to his feet. "I'll stand up and yell at you. Is that better?"

Laurie dropped the ball to the grass and put her foot on it, ignoring Connor. "Why don't I go in net first and try to block your shots, and then you can block for me, okay?" she suggested and ran for the goalposts at the far end of the field.

Alecia began dribbling, keeping her eye on the ball, gradually letting it get further and further away from her. She saw Laurie standing, poised and ready, and began running faster toward the goal. When she finally got close enough to take a shot, she let it go with everything she had, sending the black and white ball flying over Laurie's outstretched arms and through the posts.

"Good shot!" someone yelled from behind her and both Laurie and Alecia turned to see Anne and Monica standing on the sidelines beside Connor, cheering loudly.

"Hey Annie," Laurie said, scooping the ball into her arms and heading toward her. Alecia followed slowly behind, joining the others just as Anne finished introducing Monica to Laurie.

"Hello Alecia," Anne said quietly.

"Hi Anne, hi Monica," Alecia said politely, holding back slightly.

"That was some kick!" Monica cried, flipping her long, brown hair over her shoulder. "I didn't know you could kick like that."

"It isn't that big a deal," Alecia mumbled, turning red. Monica laughed and flipped her hair again. Alecia watched her, waiting for the familiar twinge of annoyance she always felt when the other girl did that. It didn't come.

"What brings you two out here?" Connor asked.

"We were just out for a walk when we passed the field and Annie said, 'Hey, isn't that Connor and Alecia and Laurie playing soccer?' And I said, 'Yeah, it looks like it.' And Annie said, 'Well, maybe we should go and say hi or something.' And of course I said, 'Definitely!' and here we are!"

Alecia felt Connor's eyes on her as Monica finished her speech, but she ignored him. She wasn't sure what was happening to her, but Monica was not annoying her the way she always had. Perhaps, just perhaps, she was beginning to change too.

"Hey, why don't you guys come play with us, we could have a mini-game!" Laurie suggested. She looked from one girl to the other, nodding.

"I don't know how to play soccer," Monica said.

"It's easy," Alecia heard herself saying. "Come play, it'll be fun."

"I'm in," Monica decided. "Hey, Connor, do you play? You and I shouldn't be on a team together. We'd lose big time against these guys, eh?" she said, dragging him away with her and Laurie.

Anne and Alecia remained where they were, looking at each other cautiously.

"Look," Alecia began, choosing her words carefully, "I'm real sorry for the way I was acting before, about Monica. I guess I was kind of jealous."

"Thanks, Leesh," Annie said quietly. "I appreciate you saying that." She smiled then, and Alecia felt a weight drop from her shoulders.

"We miss you, on the team," Alecia told her. "I miss you."

"I miss you too," Anne confessed.

They looked at each other for a minute, then Alecia kicked the ball toward her friend.

"Hey, they're waiting. Let's charge them, they'll never stop the two of us!" Alecia said and, laughing, ran out onto the field, knowing Anne was right behind her.